St. Martin's Roman Catholic Primary School

GROUND

TOILETS

MEDICAL
ROOM

FOYER

THROUGH CORRIDOR

STAFF
ROOM

CLASS
ROOM

ARY

TEMPORARY
CORRIDOR

FIRE
EXIT

FIRE
EXIT

TO HUT →

FIRST FLOOR

OFFICE

HEAD'S
OFFICE

HALL

ART
ROOM

CLASS
ROOM

CORRIDOR

CORRIDOR

CLASS
ROOM

FOYER

CLASS
ROOM

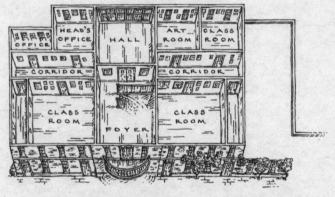

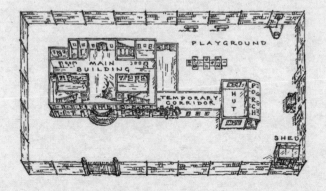

PLAYGROUND

MAIN
BUILDING

TEMPORARY
CORRIDOR

HUT

PORCH

SHED

CYNTHIA MURPHY

THE MIDNIGHT GAME

SCHOLASTIC

Published in the UK by Scholastic, 2023

Scholastic, Bosworth Avenue, Warwick, CV34 6UQ

Scholastic Ireland, 89E Lagan Road, Dublin Industrial Estate, Glasnevin, Dublin, D11 HP5F

SCHOLASTIC and associated logos are trademarks and/or
registered trademarks of Scholastic Inc.

Text © Cynthia Murphy, 2023

Map illustration by Julia Bickham © Scholastic, 2023

The moral rights of the author have been asserted by them.

ISBN 978 0702 31853 5

A CIP catalogue record for this book is available from the British Library.

Printed in the UK

Paper made from wood grown in sustainable forests and other controlled sources.

MIX

Paper | Supporting
responsible forestry

FSC® C018072

5 7 9 10 8 6

www.scholastic.co.uk

For safety or quality concerns:

UK: www.scholastic.co.uk/productinformation

EU: www.scholastic.ie/productinformation

Please be aware that some of the material in this story contains themes or events of death/dying, body horror, violence, murder and mentions of suicide.

For my little sister, Donna.
Thank you for being so proud of me.

The figure emerged from the shadows. It slunk past the playground gates, slow, almost melting into the night. Its progress was deliberate but painful. One leg dragging, a harsh, hollow wheezing emanating from its chest.

It did not look back.

Slowly, like blood trickling from a puncture wound, the figure stopped. Rested. A jangle of keys cleared the air, somehow chasing away the encroaching darkness, the horror of the night.

The figure pulled open the car door and climbed inside.

It did not look back.

It was cold in the car, and numb fingers fumbled as if on automatic, sliding the keys into the ignition and twisting until the engine reluctantly roared to life. The doors locked, a comforting click that promised safety, then the heater came on. The figure twisted the dial all the way round, relishing the white noise in its ears, and burrowed down, waiting for the air to lose its chill.

It did not look back. Instead, it pulled down the sun visor. There was no sun, of course, at almost 3:40 a.m., but there was a picture, a photograph stashed up there. In it there were two figures.

Though one of them was very definitely dead.

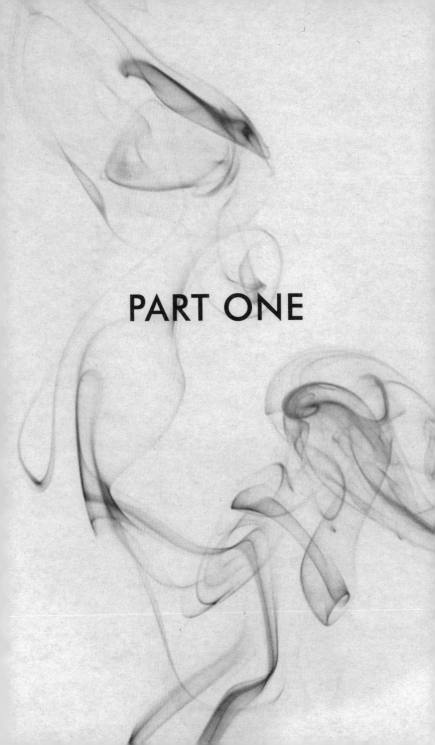

PART ONE

New thread: THE MIDNIGHT GAME

(Filters: Local area users only; Users I follow; Users who follow me)

30/06/2022   23:49

FrenchBanana: Hey, creeps. Been down a rabbit hole and came across this game, anyone ever heard of it?

Donttalktome12: Don't think so. Lemme Google real quick.

Donttalktome12: Looks sick.

YeahBoi_121: I have! Played all that stuff when I was younger – never actually played this one but totally would.

Donttalktome12: Me too.

FrenchBanana: Dunno if I would. Way too intense. And what if it was real?

HotDog45: I'm pretty sure I've heard of this or watched the movie, maybe? It's like Candyman, right?

FrenchBanana: Er, not quite.

HotDog45: Oh.

User3678: I've played this one! Utter rubbish. Don't bother. Gave up after half an hour.

FrenchBanana: Really? Would love to chat to you about your experience?

User3678: Lol, no. So boring.

FrenchBanana: OK then. Anyone else?

CreepyTeepee: I've heard of it.

FrenchBanana: Oh, yeah? Anything more to add?

01/07/2022   00:00

FrenchBanana: @CreepyTeepee?

CreepyTeepee: Sorry – just looking for something. One sec.

CreepyTeepee: This is the one, right?

Rules of the Midnight Game:
1. Do not turn on the lights

2. *Do not go to sleep*
3. *Do not leave the building*

FrenchBanana: That's the one! Question is...

Hotdog45: Who wants to play?

ELLIE

The participants approached cautiously one by one. Some arrived in cars, others on foot, but all of them were alone.

That was part of the game.

Ellie watched each of the newcomers hesitate when they arrived at the playground gate and smiled wryly because she had done the same. She had been there since eleven that evening, sitting cross-legged in a dark little alcove next to a small wooden shed. She hated being late and when she realized she was the first one there, she had thought it would be worth weighing everyone up as they arrived, see if she could try to match some faces with usernames before the game began.

A short figure pushed the gate tentatively. It swung

open with a soft squeak, and the girl smiled and took a step inside. She paused, pulled a notebook from her small messenger bag and scribbled something in it. Then she took something else out – an old-school wind-up camera, Ellie realized – and took a few snaps of the school and its compact grounds. The school building was an old one, though somehow still in use, and its presence loomed over the narrow street it was set back from. Large dark windows stared soullessly out. It was secluded here too, Ellie mused as she watched the petite girl walk around to the squat temporary classroom that sat outside the main building – "the hut", *Donttalktome12* had called it. Ellie weighed up the area once more. There were houses in running distance if she needed them, but no one close enough to hear them goofing around in there, which was good. She really didn't need a criminal record over this stupid game.

The girl and her bag disappeared into the hut as Ellie waited for the next player. She avoided looking at the vacant windows of the main building. Why were schools so much creepier when they were empty? Was this one particularly sinister because it was so old? It must be. She scanned the walls for a plaque that might give her a date but couldn't see anything in the dark. She should have brought a torch but ... you know.

Rules.

Ellie sat up straight as the next two people arrived, almost meeting at the gate simultaneously. She squinted to see a little better. A tall, blonde-haired boy dressed in a preppy shirt and jumper combo stepped back, gesturing to the gate in what he clearly thought was a gentlemanly way. The girl to his right dragged her upper lip into a sneer, her lips dark and glossy, and imitated the gesture in such a mocking way that Ellie had to hold in a laugh. A look of bewilderment creased his face as he crossed the threshold and moved closer to Ellie's hiding place. He was wearing stiff jeans and brown shoes and something about him screamed *money*. Ellie decided she would put her life on him being a private school boy. He also disappeared into the hut as the new girl lingered outside, finishing a cigarette. The end of it drooped from her lips, glued in place with gloss as she eyed up the school buildings. She dropped the butt and stretched, lithe, like a cat, before smashing the burning embers into the playground floor and marching over to the hut, her Doc Martens echoing on the asphalt.

Ellie checked her watch and hesitated – she wanted to be the last one to go in, but it was almost half past, and that was when they were supposed to be inside. She ticked people off on one hand as she kept her eyes on the gate. One – camera girl, two – preppy guy, three – goth girl. That meant there were two players left. She flicked at a hangnail as she waited and realization dawned on her – someone had to have been there before her to open the gates and the hut. Dammit. So, there was only one player left, unless they had chickened out.

No sooner had she thought it than a figure in red appeared at the gate, or rather bounced through it. This kid had way too much energy for Ellie's liking already. He tore through the playground and towards the hut, not pausing to look around first. *Impulsive*, Ellie thought. That might not end well.

Once she was sure they were all inside, Ellie stood up. Her legs were stiff from sitting on the cold, hard ground, and she brushed little pieces of gravel from the backs of her legs and denim shorts. She collected her tote bag, took stock of its contents one last time and swung it on to her shoulder, approaching the hut where they were supposed to meet. Just as she reached the bottom of the ramp that led inside, a silver glimmer caught her eye. On the playground wall, opposite the entrance, was a mirror. She walked over to it, her eyes following the lines of her reflection as it warped, swelling in odd places. She shook her head and laughed, feeling like the kids who must play here. She flipped her immaculately blow-dried hair behind one shoulder and headed up the ramp, turning back for a final glance once she reached the door.

Her reflection was back to normal.

Satisfied, Ellie threw her shoulders back, pushed open the door with her mint-green fingernails and walked into the building.

She had a game to play.

01/07/2022 00:01

FrenchBanana: Er, no, as it happens. I was going to say, *"the question is – is any of it real, or is it just creepy pasta?"* I am NOT down to play this stuff.

YeahBoi_121: I'm in! This chat is set to local peeps only, right?

HotDog45: Hell yeah! When and where?

FrenchBanana: Number 1 – no. I am not stupid enough to meet strangers off the internet. Number 2 – yes, I set the chat to local users, but only because I wanted local info on this so-called legend. Number 3 – repeat number 1. NO.

User3678: But you started this thread, right? And we're on the *d/makemebelieve* subdeddit. You MUST be a bit curious?

FrenchBanana: What? You said it was a load of rubbish a minute ago!

User3678: Nah, ignore me. I was just having you on. I've never played.

Donttalktome12: I know somewhere we can do it. Somewhere we won't be disturbed.

FrenchBanana: God, I wish my laptop had a red flag emoji for *that* comment, *@Donttalktome12…*

CreepyTeepee: Screw it. I'm in too. Can't be real, right?

HotDog45: Sweeeeeet!

YeahBoi_121: So, where we going *@Donttalktome12?*

Donttalktome12: I'll tell you when *@FrenchBanana* commits. Then they can lock the chat so it's just us.

00:07

HotDog45: They've chickened out, I reckon…

00:09

YeahBoi_121: Helllllooooooooo?

FrenchBanana: You all have to let me interview you after.

HotDog45: No worries.

YeahBoi_121: Same here.

Donttalktome12: Fine by me.

User3678: Sure, if we're stiiiiiiiiill aliiiiiiiiive…

FrenchBanana: What about you @CreepyTeepee?

CreepyTeepee: Yeah, whatever.

HotDog45: So? You in?

FrenchBanana: Fine.

User3678: Yay!

FrenchBanana: I'm going to regret this, aren't I?

MEI

The room was tiny.

Cramped and dusty like it hadn't been used for years. Maybe it hadn't, Mei thought. Maybe that was the point. *Donttalktome12* had said the building was in use, but this room clearly hadn't heard the laughter of children for a while. She counted the other figures in the room – five people now, including her. No one had spoken yet, just awkward nods and faces that screamed "what am I doing here?"

"Well, this place is a shithole."

Mei set her bag down near the door and focused on the voice, her nose wrinkling involuntarily. A tall intimidating girl sat cross-legged on a table by the whiteboard to the left

15

of the room, emanating a "don't-mess-with-me" aura and a cloud of cigarette smoke. Mei tried to catch the cough that was pushing its way up from her chest and failed miserably, letting out a pathetic little hacking sound. The girl flicked her large eyes over Mei once, rolled them to the sky and resumed flicking the lid on and off a dried-out marker pen. Mei crouched down into the corner, one hand rummaging in her bag for an inhaler. She grasped the cool plastic gratefully and took two puffs as inconspicuously as she could manage.

The room behind her stayed silent.

"Er, it's just all this dust." Mei smiled apologetically as she turned back to face the group.

"Yeah, it's pretty grim in here, right? Is this really a school?"

Mei studied the speaker – tall white guy with floppy blonde hair, at least six foot two to Mei's five foot nothing. He was wearing a polo shirt that gave off a vague impression of entitlement. Posh kid, definitely.

"This bit isn't. Well, it was, kind of, but this was a temporary classroom. The main school flooded one year and some of the kids had to have lessons in here. They're all back in the main building now, though." A skinny figure piped up from the opposite side of the room to where Mei was standing. He was leaning back against a table that had another one upturned on top of it, its legs pointing up to the ceiling. His hood was up, leaving his face mostly covered in shadow. Mei studied him carefully. Was that *Donttalktome12*? He jerked a thumb to point behind him and she noticed there was a door hidden in the shadows. Yes, he knew his way around. It was definitely him.

"It's still connected through a temporary corridor. I thought this would be a good place to start, though, since the door is wooden. No alarms, all that jazz."

Mei's skin stood on end as a cold breeze tickled her skin.

A wooden door.

They were really doing this.

"Hi, everyone!" a perky voice cut through the tension just as Mei's watch beeped its reminder. Eleven thirty. "Hope I'm not late!"

"Not at all." Mei rolled her own eyes as the lad – and he really looked like a *lad* – jumped up from behind what she assumed was the teacher's desk, to greet the final member of the group. The girl in the doorway smiled shyly and ducked her head behind a curtain of blonde hair that Taylor Swift would be proud of as the boy approached her. "You're just in time. I'm Reece—"

"I thought we weren't using real names," Mei piped up, regretting it instantly. Scary girl narrowed her eyes.

"How do *you* know that's his real name?" she purred. "He could have made it up."

"I don't… I just…"

"I don't… I just…" the girl mimicked in a high-pitched whine. "Oh, calm down. You're way too tense." She uncrossed her legs and scooted to the edge of the desk, letting her boot-clad feet brush against the worn green carpet.

"Uh-oh, she's right, though. I did use my real name." Reece shrugged, smiling at the newcomer. "Guess I'm not too good at following rules."

Mei's mouth dried up. That was not a good start.

"I'm Ellie." The blonde girl smiled. "I guess we would find out anyway, right? I mean, we have to write our names down. For the ritual."

"That's true," Scary girl agreed. "I'm Toni."

"Hugo," posh boy offered, one meaty hand in the air. "Hugo Winstan—"

"First names only, genius," Toni snarled. She fixed her eyes on Mei. "You?"

"I'm Mei," she managed to say, words tumbling from her mouth in a hurry. "Like the month, just spelled differently. It's Chinese, I'm half Chinese…" She bit her lip, hoping it would stop her nervous rambling. Her voice was smaller than she'd liked. She hadn't thought she'd be so scared.

"And I'm Callum," the skinny boy in the hoodie spoke up. He approached the rest of the group and placed a bundle in the centre of an empty table. Dull golden drawing pins, a fistful of torn paper, and six pencils all in varying degrees of falling apart, scattered across the hard surface. "Are you ready to play?"

01/07/2022   06:30

YeahBoi_121: How we all feeling this bright and sunny morning?

HotDog45: WTF? What time is it?

YeahBoi_121: Half six, just having breakfast.

YeahBoi_121: Take it you're not an early riser.

HotDog45: Fell asleep with my headphones in. Didn't realize I had such a loud alert for this thread. Shit me up.

06:32

FrenchBanana: Lol. Someone butt-dialled me once when I was asleep with pods in. Scared the life out of me.

YeahBoi_121: Morning @FrenchBanana. You still on for our adventure?

FrenchBanana: Suppose so.

User3678: They can't WAIT ;)

FrenchBanana: I'm about to do a bit of research this morning actually. Gotta get the bus to school and it takes FOR EVER.

User3678: School? How old are you?

CreepyTeepee: Wait – this is a good point.

YeahBoi_121: Morning @User3678 and @CreepyTeepee. Almost the whole gang.

06:34

Donttalktome12: I'm here. Not fully awake, but here.

YeahBoi_121: Morning @Donttalktome12

FrenchBanana: Stop being so cheerful @YeahBoi_121, it's weird.

YeahBoi_121: Soz. Just being polite.

FrenchBanana: @User3678??? @CreepyTeepee??? What do you mean? What's a good point?

FrenchBanana: Hellllllooooo. I need to go soon!

User3678: Isn't it obvious? Frenchy told us they went to school. Which means they're sixteen – or younger.

CreepyTeepee: Exactly. None of us actually know each other, do we? What if one of us is lying?

HotDog45: About what?

CreepyTeepee: Oh, I dunno. Age. Motivation. *Bad intentions.* I mean, we're agreeing to meet up at midnight in God-knows-where. It's a bit dodge, isn't it?

YeahBoi_121: Nah, I don't believe that. Surely we're all good eggs.

User3678: Good eggs? How old are *you* @YeahBoi_121?

FrenchBanana: Lol. I guess you're right, though.

FrenchBanana: None of you are murderers or human traffickers, right?

21

06:40

FrenchBanana: RIGHT?!

06:42

Donttalktome12: No, we're just a gang of good eggs who are talking about summoning a demon...

06:44

HotDog45: A WHAT?

HotDog45: I'm sorry, I must still be dreaming. Who said anything about a DEMON???

FrenchBanana: Someone hasn't done their research...

HotDog45: You literally just said you didn't yet either!

FrenchBanana: Of course I have. A bit, anyway.

CreepyTeepee: You didn't even search it on here after our chat last night @HotDog45?

HotDog45: No ... did everyone else?

User3678: Yep.

YeahBoi_121: Me too.

Donttalktome12: Same. Wanted to know what we were getting ourselves into.

HotDog45: Damn. I was too tired.

06:50

FrenchBanana: So we're all off to … school, or wherever today, right?

06:51

FrenchBanana: For the record, I was sixteen last month.

FrenchBanana: Anyone else up for sharing their personal details?

06:55

FrenchBanana: OKKKKKKK … right. Gotta run.

CreepyTeepee: I'm seventeen :)

23

YeahBoi_121: Eighteen here.

HotDog45: Yeah, I'm eighteen too.

User3678: Seventeen. What about you @Donttalktome12?

Donttalktome12: I'm the baby along with @FrenchBanana. In my last year of school.

FrenchBanana: Guess we have to meet up to see who's lying...

HotDog45: We could send pics.

User3678: Yeah, cos those can't be faked.

FrenchBanana: I really have to go! @HotDog45, do your research!

Donttalktome12: We're chatting later, right? I might have news on a venue...

CreepyTeepee: Yeah, I'm back late. Say eight-ish?

FrenchBanana: Good for me! Bye, guys.

HotDog45: Me too, see ya!

Donttalktome12: Sound.

User3678: Can barely wait.

06:59

YeahBoi_121: Has everyone gone?

07:00

YeahBoi_121: See you later.

CALLUM

Callum swept his eyes around the barely lit room and swallowed – hard. The security lights mounted over the doorway did nothing apart from cast unnatural shadows over the other faces in the room. It was definitely too late to back out now.

Right?

"Where did you get all this stuff?" The small girl – Mei – trailed her fingers across the ragtag selection of pencils he had collected.

"Just around the room," he gestured to the temporary cabin, or the hut as his mum called it. "There were loads of random pencil pots still lying around so I rummaged through them. Same with the rest." He gestured to the shreds of lined paper. "Ripped those from an old exercise book I found in a cupboard and the pins are from a display board."

"They don't look very sharp," Toni mused, picking one up with her chipped, black nails. Callum gave her a quick once-over while she wasn't looking; he took in the silver pendant around her neck. It was strung from a thin chain, classic looking, which seemed completely at odds with the rest of her outfit.

"Or very hygienic," the blonde boy – Hugo, Callum reminded himself – piped up. "No offence."

Callum's lip twitched and he bit back a smirk. "None taken. I was here early to open up, so had a nosy around while I was waiting. Take it or leave it." He slid himself on to the desk next to his stuff. "So, everyone still down for this?"

The room fell silent for a second.

"Hell yeah." Reece laughed and the air seemed to lighten a little. "I can't wait to sneak around this place. I've not been in a primary school since … well, since I went to one."

"It's nothing special, hate to tell you." Callum laughed back, the other boy's excitement infectious. "It is pretty big in there, though. In fact…" He slid from his spot and walked over to the teacher's desk, pulling a laminated sheet from the wall with a soft pop as the ancient Blu-Tack detached itself. "Here."

"What is it?" Mei asked.

"Floor plan." Callum put the sheet on top of the pencils and pointed to an area that was shaded red. "It's a fire safety thing – there's one in every room. They're usually by the door, sometimes near the teacher's desk. But this red bit shows where you are, and the arrows point you to the nearest fire exit."

"Not much help if we can't leave the building," the blonde girl muttered. Ellie? God, he wished these people had name badges.

"True," he conceded, "but they'll be useful if you find yourself lost."

"Or worse," whispered Mei, "trapped."

Another second of silence.

"Anyway," Callum tried to inject some level of confidence into his voice, "it's just a heads-up, you know. Hopefully we'll stick to the plan, stay together. I know my way around. But just in case you do get lost," he tapped the laminate with a bitten nail, "these should help you get your bearings."

"Great," Hugo boomed, making Ellie jump, which sent a ripple of laughter through the group. "Sorry," he winced.

"Don't be," Ellie smiled, putting one hand on his arm. Callum could see his face turn red, even though the room was dark. "I'm just a bit nervous, you know? But I'm sure we'll all look out for each other." She squeezed his arm and Hugo's chest puffed out ever so slightly.

"Definitely," he agreed.

Callum bit back a laugh and cleared his throat. "Shall we go over the rules one more time?" He pushed up the thick cuffed sleeve of his hooded jacket and squinted down at a heavy digital watch. "It's eleven forty, so we have time. I reckon as long as we start at five to midnight, that gives us time to do everything."

"Maybe ten to?" Mei chipped in as she fished around in her backpack. "Just in case?"

"Fine by me." Callum looked at each person in turn. Ellie smiled shyly and nodded, which meant that Hugo and Reece, who both had their eyes glued to her, did the same. He moved his attention over to Toni, who just looked bored at the entire proceeding.

"Yeah, whatever," she said, before turning her attention to Mei, who was now flipping through the pages of a reporter's notebook, absorbed in her task. "What are you looking for, brainiac?"

"The rules," Mei answered, unfazed by the snide name. "I wrote down everything I could find about the game and turned it into a list of rules. Ah, here they are!" She started to pull pages from the pad, the wire at the top tearing through the perforated edges with a dry whisper. "I copied them out for each of us. You know, since we can't have our phones to check."

"Such a pick me," Toni muttered, but the rest of the

29

group drowned her out with their thanks. Callum made a mental note not to get stuck in a room alone with Toni. The sarcasm would kill him before anything else did.

"Ready?" Mei cleared her throat and began to read aloud. "Rules of The Midnight Game. Rule one…"

"What time is it?"

Callum saw Mei's cheeks flush ever-so-slightly at Toni's interruption.

"Rude," Hugo mumbled, but Mei smiled tightly.

"It's fine," she said evenly. "Callum, what time is it now?"

He checked his watch again, silently agreeing with Hugo. "Eleven forty-two. Two minutes later than the last time I said."

Toni stretched, sticking out her black-clad legs from her seated position on the table. "I'm going out for a cigarette. We *can* still do that, right, Miss Rules?"

"Until midnight, yes."

"Wonderful," Toni sneered. "Feel free to carry on without me." She let her heavy boots thump on to the hollow floor and stomped over to the doorway. The whole cabin shook with each step, as if its thin frame had forgotten what it was like to have living, breathing human beings inside its walls.

"Oh, we will," Callum heard Reece, the sporty-looking, energetic dude, mutter, before he passed a sheet of the rules over to Ellie, who twinkled back at him, much to Hugo's annoyance.

Toni was clearly not the fan favourite in this group.

"So, where were we?" Hugo accepted a sheet from Mei and scanned the page. "Rule one…"

"Oh, wait," Ellie interrupted him, looking over to the windows. "We should wait until Toni gets back."

Reece snorted a laugh. "What? Why? She's been nothing but a b—"

Ellie cut him off. "Because it's fair, that's why. Would you leave me in the dark like that?"

"No, but you're … nice," Reece finished weakly. Callum watched the faces of the others as he finally relented. "Fine. Let's give her until quarter to. If she hasn't finished her smoke break in two minutes, we start without her. Yeah?"

"Fine with me," Callum agreed. Hugo and Mei nodded their agreement as Ellie smiled at him and mouthed "thank you".

Callum pulled his legs up on to the table and crossed them, watching the others.

And waiting.

01/07/2022   12:42

FrenchBanana: Hey guys, anyone around?

12:44

YeahBoi_121: I am.

CreepyTeepee: Yeah, me too. On my lunch break. What's up?

FrenchBanana: Oh, nothing up. Just trying to do some research and can't find much. Think it's definitely a creepy pasta. You guys?

CreepyTeepee: Not had time yet. Tonight's job.

YeahBoi_121: Same.

FrenchBanana: Oh. OK. Well, send some links if you do come across anything?

CreepyTeepee: Sure.

YeahBoi_121: Ditto.

FrenchBanana: Thanks.

12:57

Donttalktome12: Hey @*FrenchBanana*, you still online?

12:58

FrenchBanana: Hey! Yeah, not got long, though.

Donttalktome12: Thought this might interest you…

Donttalktome12: https:/ThePrestfieldTimes.com/localnews/ crime/girl.found.dea…

FrenchBanana: What did I say about red flag behaviour?

FrenchBanana: What's this got to do with TMG?

Donttalktome12: Just read it. Gotta run.

13:03

FrenchBanana: @*Donttalktome12* you still there???

FrenchBanana: HOLY SHIT.

FrenchBanana: Guys, you need to read this. I've gotta get back to class but ... Jesus.

TONI

Toni glared back at the hut through sore eyes. Whatever eyeliner she had chosen that night was starting to burn, irritating her tear ducts. Cheap shite. The smoke didn't help either, but she took another long, luxurious drag anyway, pulling the toxins deep into her bloodstream before expelling a cloud of noxious grey. She studied her fingers, chipped nails stained yellow by the nicotine. She should really quit; it was a disgusting habit, but at times like these, it was the only thing that kept her calm.

She took one final pull, the only sound in the darkness that of the cigarette paper being eaten alive by the burning embers. It was bitter and she winced as the heat hit her lungs, but the process calmed her nerves, and once she was grinding the end into the gravel of the playground, she felt much better. Ready to go back and join the random group assembled in the cabin.

She headed back inside, sliding her hand into the pocket of her short black pinafore dress. All black tonight, down to her long sleeves and tights. All the better to hide from the Midnight Man, surely. Not like that tit, Ellie, with her bright blonde hair and summer clothes. Or Reece in his luminous red tracksuit. *Idiot*. They were going to stick out like the proverbial sore thumb. Ah well, not her problem. Toni climbed back on to the rickety porch and pushed open the door with one hand, easing a tablet of gum out of the packet in her pocket with the other. She popped it into her mouth before entering.

"Rule one…"

"You started without me!" Toni interrupted dramatically. The rest of the group turned to look at her and she sniggered. "Oh, please, what's this? A séance?" They had moved to sit on the floor in her absence, forming a circle in front of the door that led into the rest of the building.

"Sorry, I … we did wait, but…" the little geeky one started to stutter and Toni realized the rest of the group were staring daggers at her. Oops, she seemed to have riled everyone up before the game had even started.

"Joking, joking," Toni held her hands up in surrender. "I'm not bothered, really."

"Come on, sit down over here. Hugo, move up one,

will you?" Blondie patted a space next to her on the floor, her bright nails looking out of place against the threadbare carpet. Toni waited as Hugo refused to look at her before reluctantly shuffling over, making a space for her. "We waited for you." Ellie looked around the circle. "We wanted to make sure it was fair."

"Er, OK." Toni dropped to her knees and tried not to wince. The carpet might be almost non-existent, but what was left angrily rubbed the skin of her knees through her tights. She pointed at the small girl. Was she wearing a Pokémon T-shirt? Good God. "Go on then, er—"

"Mei," she supplied, handing Toni the final sheet of paper. "And you're welcome."

Oooh. Feistier than she looks. Toni cracked a smile.

"Let's start again. I'll read the first one and we can go around the circle." Mei took the lead and Toni sat back. She might as well listen since they'd waited for her. "*Rule one: do not turn on the lights.* This includes lighters, phones and any electronics. Matches are the only thing allowed." She turned to her left. "Callum?"

Callum cleared his throat. "*Rule two: do not go to sleep.*"

"As if you would be tempted to." Ellie giggled.

"Right?" Callum laughed. "Just going to take a quick nap while being stalked by a dem—"

"*Don't* say the word," Mei warned, her voice serious. "We have enough going on without getting haunted by,

37

well, by more than we bargained for." She glanced around the circle. "Hugo?"

"*Rule three: do not go outside or leave the building.*" He paused. "Wait, I meant to ask this before – if we go out there" – he nodded to the flimsy wooden door – "aren't we leaving the building?"

Callum flipped his hood down and scratched at his head, revealing a short, tight afro. "I don't think so. Technically it's all part of the school, right? I only chose this bit because it was easier to break into than the main door. I have the keys for the inside doors, so I can let us in at the end of the corridor, but the big main one is alarmed. If I'd smashed that one in, it would've contacted the police straight away."

Toni sighed. Was he serious? "Then won't exactly the same thing happen when you open this door?"

"Nope. The alarm is only triggered if the front door or a window is opened – there's nothing inside the building to set it off, no sensors or anything. I'll turn it off anyway. I found out the code just in case."

"You're sure?" Toni asked.

"A hundred per cent. I've done it before." Callum turned back to face Hugo. "So, to get back to your question, that door leads to a temporary corridor. It's flimsy, but it's enclosed and leads to another door that will take us into the main building. I figured since it's all connected, it's classed as the same building." He looked around the circle. "Right?"

"Yeah," Toni shrugged. She wished they'd just get on with it. "My turn now? OK. *Rule four: do not carry a weapon. This is for your own safety.* Jeez, Mei, dramatic much?"

"Well, you saw that article, didn't you?"

"Yeah." A chill ran down Toni's spine and she shivered despite herself. "I did. OK, fine. Ellie's turn."

"*Rule five:*" Ellie said softly, shifting her hair behind her shoulder, "*if your candle blows out, you must re-light it in ten seconds.* If you can't, you must surround yourself with a circle of salt. If you don't..."

"We know," Toni snapped. She wanted another cigarette. "He'll get you." It was supposed to come out as a joke, but she barely cleared a whisper. The air around the circle crackled with tension for a moment.

"Reece?" Ellie smiled at the boy in red.

"*Rule six: move. Don't stay in one place for too long.*" He gestured to the list where there was one final rule. "Mei? You want to finish?"

"OK. *Rule seven: you must play until 3:33 a.m.* That's when the Midnight Man will leave, and you will be free."

"OK." Toni rolled her shoulders back and forced a savage grin. "Who's ready to play?"

Greater Manchester news > Prestbury news > Crime

SAD SUICIDE OF MISSING GIRL, 16, IN "RITUAL GAME"

"A devastating loss and a stark reminder to reach out for help when you need it."

By Jessica Johnson

The inquest into the "ritualistic" death of a teenage girl whose body was found in a derelict cinema has given a ruling of suicide.

Alice Gooding, 16, of Tempus Street, was last seen on the evening of 31st October 2021. Her body was discovered in the derelict building three days later. The multiplex has since been demolished.

But the inquest heard that Alice's body was discovered in a small cleaning cupboard near the main entrance of the cinema by local "urban explorer", Luke Dawson. The police report stated that the small glass panel in the door had been smashed from the outside. When her body was discovered, Alice had been sat cross-legged on the floor inside a circle of salt. There was glass in her hair, and she held a burnt-out candle. Several used matches were scattered on the floor around her.

Police confirmed at the time that they were not treating the death as suspicious, despite the circumstances that were described by Mr Dawson as almost "like some kind of ritual". However, Dr Phillips gave the cause of death as sudden cardiac arrest, which was the result of self-inflicted wounds.

A statement from Alice's family said: "The passing of our bright, beautiful Alice has broken our hearts. We wish that she had found the strength to talk to us, rather than feeling that this was her only way out. Not seeing her smiling face every day is a devastating loss, and a stark reminder to reach out for help when you need it. We thank you for respecting our privacy at this difficult time."

Coroner Grayson de Bruyne said: "Although the circumstances surrounding Alice's death appear sinister, and there has been speculation in the community, given the medical report and the assurance that police are not looking for anyone in connection with the death, I am ruling her death as suicide. This is a tragic loss and I offer my condolences to her family at this sad time."

HUGO

Hugo turned the paper over in his hands, running one finger along the ragged edge. Why exactly were his palms so clammy? He was desperate to take a deep breath but not while there were five pairs of eyes on him. He would not show even a smidge of weakness. He had been brought up better than that.

"You OK, Hugo?" He tried to arrange his face into a look of easy nonchalance, but he could smell the faint minty tang of Ellie's chewing gum as she leaned over him. Her bare arm grazed his leg, and he suppressed a shiver as goosebumps exploded down his back. My goodness, she was pretty.

"Er, yes, of course I am." Her big brown eyes didn't

look convinced, so he wracked his brain for an excuse. "I'm just a little concerned" – he grimaced before holding the paper in the air – "about remembering all of the rules."

"What do you mean?" Mei asked, her delicate features scrunched in a frown behind her glasses. "Do you need to go over them again? I thought I'd made them really clear?"

"You have. You did a wonderful job," he reassured her. "It's not that." Hugo cleared his throat, nervous now. "It's my ... I mean, I have..."

"Yes? What have you got, preppy? Aside from a trust-fund," Toni prompted, her voice bored. He studied her carefully and saw that her eyes were twinkling like she was making a joke. She was hard to read and kind of pretty too, but in a *don't-mess-with-me-or-I'll-punch-you-in-the-mouth* kind of way. She scared him a little bit – not that he'd ever admit that. Winstanleys weren't scared of anything or anyone, so his grandfather had said, anyway. Hugo took a deep breath, puffed out his chest and forced his shoulders back.

"ADHD," he blurted, fixing his eyes back on Mei. He took a deep, wobbly breath. "I have recently been diagnosed with ADHD and I have trouble remembering certain things, especially when I get given new information. What if I forget the rules?"

"Oh." Mei smiled in relief, pushing her glasses back up her nose. "You can take it with you. That's why I wrote out six pages, so we could all keep our own copy."

"Oh. Great!" Hugo's heart rate slowed again as he repeated himself. "Great, that was very thoughtful of you, Mei. Thank you." He folded the page over and slid it into the pocket of his jeans. Ellie gave him a reassuring smile and squeezed his forearm. Good. He didn't have to remember them all, he could just pull the list out when he needed it.

"It's ten to," Callum said quietly. The group's eyes drifted to the pile of pencils in the middle of the circle. "We should get started now if we want to do this properly."

Hugo swallowed hard.

What had possessed him?

"Let's get this show on the road!" The chavvy bloke, Reece, rubbed his hands together in glee as the hair on Hugo's arms lifted. He suddenly had a very bad feeling about this. Did everyone else feel the same way?

"Get your stuff together and let's do it at the same time," Mei suggested, already on her feet. The rest of the group moved a little slower, seemingly unfazed, until it was just him and Ellie left on the carpet. He watched the others as they started to discuss the best way to prick their fingers, his vision going slightly fuzzy as his mouth became dry.

"Are you sure you're OK?" Ellie asked. Her brow was furrowed and she tilted her head to one side as she studied his face. "There's still time to back out, you know. You don't have to play."

"It's not that," Hugo tugged at the collar of his polo

44

shirt, as if it would ease the lump in his throat. He had started to perspire now, the thick cotton under his arms dampening slightly. "I … erm…" he pulled at the collar again, his voice barely audible. "Oh, God. I was hoping this wouldn't happen."

"What would happen?" Ellie asked. She was watching him through narrow eyes. "Are you having a panic attack or something?"

"Or something," Hugo said, wincing at the sound of his croaky voice. "It's just that … well…"

"Yes?" Ellie urged.

"I don't like blood."

01/07/2022   15:57

YeahBoi_121: Fridayyyyyyyy, am I right?

User3678: According to the calendar, yes.

YeahBoi_121: Lol

User3678: Wasn't a joke.

FrenchBanana: All right you two. So, who read the article?

15:59

FrenchBanana: No one?

16:01

FrenchBanana: Seriously??

YeahBoi_121: Just read it. Poor girl. Suicide really isn't the answer.

CreepyTeepee: Oh, please. That's the last thing someone

46

in that amount of despair needs to hear. Sometimes it feels like the only way out.

User3678: Speaking from experience, @CreepyTeepee?

16:04

User3678 deleted their comment.

User3678: I'm sorry. That was harsh.

Donttalktome12: What did I miss?

CreepyTeepee: Nothing.

FrenchBanana: We were talking about the article you sent before. About the girl who died playing The Midnight Game.

HotDog45: Hey guys! How you all doing? We settle a date for this thing yet?

FrenchBanana: Good point.

FrenchBanana: Right – let's look at everything. We have to:

User3678: I feel a list coming on…

YeahBoi_121: I love a list.

Donttalktome12: Same.

FrenchBanana: 1. Discuss above article. 2. Decide a time and place. 3. Gather our resources.

Donttalktome12: I have #2 sorted. The place, anyway.

FrenchBanana: Really? Where?

Donttalktome12: A primary school. I know where I can get the keys. Loads of space to walk around in – better than doing it in a house I reckon. Plus, no parents.

YeahBoi_121: Cool.

CreepyTeepee: Creepy, more like.

HotDog45: Assumed you liked creepy, @CreepyTeepee.

CreepyTeepee: I do … in theory…

FrenchBanana: OK, we have a venue. What about a date?

Donttalktome12: Weekend would be best. A Saturday so there definitely won't be anyone around.

HotDog45: What about tomorrow?

FrenchBanana: Seriously? So soon?

YeahBoi_121: I have a thing but could probably swing by after.

Donttalktome12: I was just gonna be online all night. I'm in.

FrenchBanana: OK. I have to sneak out anyway. Might as well get it over with.

HotDog45: Ha, me too. I'm technically grounded.

FrenchBanana: I'm pretty sure I don't want to know why... So that's four of us. What about you guys, @User3678 and @CreepyTeepee?

CreepyTeepee: I'll have to rearrange some stuff. I'm meant to be staying at a friend's. Sure I can switch it though.

16:13

FrenchBanana: @User3678? You game?

User3678: Some of us have lives, you know.

HotDot45: Come onnnnnnnn.

Donttalktome12: Yeah, @User3678 – put your money where your mouth is.

16:16

User3678: Fine.

YeahBoi_121: Yesssss. So, we have a place, what about a time? Half an hour before midnight?

Donttalktome12: Sound. Should be enough time. I'll stick the address on after.

FrenchBanana: Great, that's number two checked off the list. Number one can wait a minute – what about number three? The resources?

HotDog45: What do you mean by resources?

CreepyTeepee: They mean the stuff we need to do it. You know, candles, paper…

YeahBoi_121: Salt.

FrenchBanana: Yeah, that stuff.

HotDog45: Ah, right, I get you now. So, what do we need?

REECE

What he wouldn't give to have a girl like that Ellie leaning over him and soothing his worries away. Reece eyed the pair still sat on the floor, a tiny bud of jealousy unravelling in his stomach. Her lush hair brushed Hugo's bare forearm and Reece almost shivered, imagining it was him. Man, she was hot.

"We ready or what?" Reece refocused his attention on Mei, the tiny girl who appeared to be the boss of this motley crew. She wore such a serious expression behind her little wire-rimmed glasses, totally out of sorts with her cartoon top and leggings.

She looked about twelve as she checked her watch. "We don't have much time left, if we still want to do this?" she said.

"Yeah, get moving lovebirds." The words were out of Reece's mouth before he could stop himself. Ellie shot him a filthy look.

"As if that's the first thing on anyone's mind," Mei tutted.

"Oh, I don't know," Toni purred, passing behind Reece so closely that he could feel her warm breath on his neck, smell the tang of stale cigarette smoke. "Being scared makes me kind of horny."

The others formed a semi-circle around the door into the main building and Callum let out a snort of laughter.

"You" – he pointed at Toni with the tiny stub of a pencil – "are terrifying."

"Thank you." She grinned at him, her teeth wolfish. "I try."

"Come on!" All eyes flicked to Mei again. There was a red band of frustration running across her cheeks and nose and her voice was strained. "We need to hurry up. Banter all you want to after midnight."

"Agreed." Callum smiled at her. "OK, we all have watches?"

A chorus of yeses accompanied six wrists raised in the air.

"Now we need the pencil, piece of paper and something to prick your finger with." Mei gestured to the neat pile laid on her bag. "I have some sterilized sewing needles if anyone wants one. Otherwise, use what you've got."

Reece reached forwards and took one of the needles, followed by Callum and Toni. He tapped the sharp end absent-mindedly, pressing his fingertip against it with enough pressure for the skin to dimple but not break. When he looked back up, posh boy Hugo was watching him and looked a decidedly pale greyish colour. "Hugo?" He offered, removing the needle and tipping it so the light from outside glinted on the sharp end. "You want one?" To Reece's delight he turned slightly more green than grey. "Ellie? What about you?"

"I'm all set, thanks." She was rooting through a heavy-looking tote bag that had some affirmational quote splashed across the side. She's cute, Reece thought, but probably not very clever. She pulled out a black case triumphantly and set it on the floor in front of Hugo. It was about the size of one of those tin pencil cases he'd had at school, the kind that's full of rulers and other Maths stuff. He had only ever used the compass to pierce holes in the lid, though.

"What's that?" Hugo asked as Ellie opened the case. She pried out a small, black piece of plastic and held it out towards him. From what Reece could see it was the size and shape of a marker pen. She uncapped it, pressed the nib end on to the tip of her outstretched finger and smiled. There was a quiet click and when she pulled it away a dark bead of blood appeared on her index finger.

She smeared it on to a piece of paper before popping it into her mouth.

"Finger pricker," she said, removing her finger. Reece tried not to stare. "It's actually called a lancing device, but that hardly rolls off the tongue when you're having a hypo." She shrugged at the blank look on Hugo's face. "Hypoglycaemia? It means my blood sugar is low. I'm diabetic. I do it all the time."

"You do? Did it hurt?" Hugo eyed her curiously.

"Not a bit." She went back into her bag and pulled out another, sealed in plastic. "This one's spare and sterile. Here." Reece turned away, pricking his own finger as Ellie delicately tended to the rich kid. He pushed the needle in, gritting his teeth as he heard her murmur soothing words. There was a click and a soft cheer from Ellie as Hugo breathed an audible sigh of relief. Reece fought the urge to pull a face; instead he watched his own blood spill down his finger. He'd gone in way too deep with that needle. He quickly smeared it across the paper and wiped it on his hoodie, hoping no one would notice. It was already red after all.

"All done?" said Mei.

"Yep. What now? Names?" Callum asked.

Mei nodded. "Yes – first only. Middle if you really want, I guess, but no surnames. The Midnight Man needs to know whose blood he's tasting."

"Gross," Ellie whispered.

The faint scratch of pencil on paper filled the room as they signed their souls away. Reece suppressed a laugh as he scrawled his name on to the paper – even he was leaning into the dramatics.

"Is that it?" Ellie asked as she got to her feet. "Don't we need to write the other bit – you know, the secret?"

"Oh, yeah, either your awful secret or the real reason you're here." Callum grabbed a discarded sheet of paper from one of the desks and quickly ripped it into pieces, handing it out. "Quickly. Write it down and put it somewhere safe. You have to keep this one."

Reece curled a hand around his piece, committing the reason he was there to paper. He folded it up as small as it would go and slid it inside his jacket pocket, patting it for good measure.

"Right then." Mei tucked her roll of paper into a little pocket on the waistband of her leggings. "Don't lose those. You'll need them to end the game."

A chorus of murmured assent echoed around the room as Mei walked over to stand in front of the door. She held a small, red candle in one hand and a box of long matches in the other, the kind Reece had seen his dad light the barbecue with. "It's almost time. Grab everything you want to bring with you and be ready to light your candle from this one. We won't be coming back."

"Wait, we have to stick our names to the door before we do anything," Callum interrupted, holding out a handful of pins. "That's what these are for."

"Oh, of course, sorry." Mei tried – and failed – to smile. "I'm a bit nervous."

"Don't worry." Callum held out his hand and they all took one of the dull brass pins from him. Reece watched as he joined Mei and put a reassuring hand on her shoulder. "The door's pretty hollow, I think. These should go right in."

Reece hung back, watching as the others approached the door. They were already forming alliances without him. A line of torn paper danced before his eyes, each piece scrawled with a first name and a smear of dark red blood. He swallowed, approaching slowly and pinning his to the bottom as a thrill of excitement coursed through him. No going back now.

"All done," he said loudly, shoving the tack in with a flourish, before pushing the sleeves of his jacket up to expose pale forearms. "Now what?"

"Now we perform the ritual," Toni spoke up. Even her voice tremored slightly. "Right? Now we call the Midnight Man."

"Yes, we do." Mei wiped her palms across the sides of her leggings before taking hold of the box of matches. She removed one and her hand trembled so violently the match fell to the floor as the others rattled like old, dried bones in a coffin. "Sorry" – her voice was hoarse – "didn't realize I was so nervous."

"Here." Toni took the box of matches and struck one expertly. The flame smoked for a second as she held it to the red candle, the brand-new wick catching slowly and then all at once with a hiss. "Ready?"

Mei swallowed hard as Reece watched, entranced. "Ready."

d/makemebelieve

01/07/2022   16:19

FrenchBanana: Everyone needs to bring their own kit, is that OK?

User3678: How come?

FrenchBanana: Well, I imagine we'll get split up at some point. You don't want to get stuck without your own candle, do you?

YeahBoi_121: Why not? Will something spooooooooooky happen?

FrenchBanana: Seriously, did no one do their research?

16:21

CreepyTeepee: *Insert tumbleweed gif*

16:23

FrenchBanana: Fine. I'll tell you in a minute.

FrenchBanana: Right, copy and paste this somewhere, please. You're going to need:

* A candle, preferably a tall one that will last and is easy to carry.
* Matches. NOT a lighter, ONLY matches.
* Salt – enough to draw a thick circle around you if you need it.

CreepyTeepee: Is that it?

FrenchBanana: Yep, apart from the pencil and stuff. I'll bring the red candle to start the ritual; we only need one of those.

YeahBoi_121: Seems easy enough, thanks *@FrenchBanana*.

Donttalktome12: Got it, cheers.

16:26

FrenchBanana: You got that *@User3678* and *@HotDog45*?

16:27

HotDog45: Sorry, gaming at same time. Yeah, got it.

16:30

FrenchBanana: *@User3678*?

User3678: Yehyeh, got it.

FrenchBanana: Great. Remember, you MUST have your own stuff.

YeahBoi_121: You said you'd tell us why, remember?

FrenchBanana: I'm getting to it. First, did everyone read that article?

HotDog45: Yeah. Wait, one sec.

HotDog45: Pretty rough, right? You think she played the game and got so freaked out she topped herself?

Donttalktome12: Er, dunno if that's the politically correct way to say that.

HotDog45: Say what?

Donttalktome12: That she completed suicide.

HotDog45: Oh. Right.

HotDog45: Well, do you? Think she was scared into it?

CreepyTeepee: Maybe. But none of this is real, right?

FrenchBanana: Right...

User3678: Wait a minute – so you think this girl played the game and scared herself silly? Scared herself enough to take her own life?

Donttalktome12: I mean, maybe. We don't know how stable she was beforehand, do we?

HotDog45: I guess not.

YeahBoi_121: Or...

16:33

YeahBoi_121: Or...

FrenchBanana: Go on, I'll bite. Or what, @YeahBoi_121?

YeahBoi_121: Or the Midnight Man is real. And he killed her.

ELLIE

What was it about fire? Ellie's eyes tracked the quivering flame as she tried to curb her fight or flight response. What the hell was she doing here? This was ridiculous. It wasn't too late to rip her name off the door, destroy that and the paper that kept her secret before the ritual was complete. She could burn it right now – hell, she could eat it if she had to. Anything to keep her out of the running.

Instead, she watched the flame twist and grow along with the unease inside of her.

"What's next?" Even Callum's voice was shaky now. Poor Mei had gone a sickly shade, her glasses casting large shadows over the hollows of her eyes. She looked like some macabre cartoon character, her features strangely exaggerated in the light.

"We knock." Mei's voice barely hit a whisper, so she cleared her throat.

Ellie flicked her eyes over the rest of the group and saw that the candlelight made everyone look as ghoulish as Mei did, a cast of Tim Burton characters standing there in the gloom. Gooseflesh erupted all down her arms and she wished she had brought a jumper with her. Maybe she'd find one inside, or one of the boys would lend her something. "We knock," Mei repeated, clearer this time. "Twenty-two times. The last one has to be at exactly midnight, or it won't work."

"So let's do it slowly from one minute to?" Hugo said from Ellie's left. She was surprised – it was the most useful he'd been so far. She smiled encouragingly at him, and he ducked his head slightly, cheeks darkening.

"Good idea." Callum nodded. "Everyone got their stuff? And their, er, motivation?" He tapped the zipped pocket of his jacket as everyone else checked for their second piece of paper. All heads bobbed in agreement. There was silence otherwise, apart from the spit and hiss of the flame. Ellie surreptitiously tapped the underside of her bra, the hiding place that had yet to fail her. It wasn't going to fall out of there in a hurry.

"Good. Right, Mei." Callum looked down at the small girl and she nodded. Ellie's stomach knotted itself together.

"We need to start in a sec."

"Right." She took a deep shaking breath and pushed it out slowly so as not to bother the flame, her mouth a small o. "Make sure you have your candles ready. I'll blow this one out after the last knock. When I relight it, you all have to light yours from it before we can go through the door. OK?"

More nods.

More silence.

"Go," Callum whispered.

"One," Mei said, rapping her knuckles on the door. She looked to Callum for reassurance and Ellie saw him nod, his eyes crinkling kindly.

"Two," he joined in as Mei knocked a second time. "Three. Four. Five."

The hollow knocking swelled, filling the room. Ellie sucked in a deep breath as a gust of wind scorched her bare arms.

"Wh … what was that?" Mei stuttered as the flame danced wildly in the breeze.

"Six." Callum chimed and she managed a knock. "Don't get distracted. Seven." He was nodding his head to each number, keeping Mei on task. Ellie was glad to be an observer right now; she didn't think she'd be able to keep it together like he was doing. He seemed like someone who would be calm in a crisis. She put that thought away for later. A quick glance around showed that everyone

else stood transfixed, their heads bobbing too. "Eight."
"Nine." Six voices chimed this time. It broke the tension a
little and the muscles in Ellie's neck relaxed slightly. "Ten.
Eleven…"

"Halfway," Reece whispered, tugging at the zipper on
his jacket. Ellie studied him carefully. He didn't seem so
confident now.

"Twelve." The gust of wind ripped through the little
cabin again, whipping the ends of Ellie's hair, but Mei was
ready for it, her small hand wrapped around the flame to
protect it.

"What is that?" Toni hissed, shivering visibly.

"Thirteen."

"A draft, maybe?" Ellie heard herself saying, even
though she wasn't sure she believed it. No one responded.
"Fourteen," she echoed the others.

Ellie began to shiver. It seemed to start from her feet,
her legs shaking slightly in her denim shorts, goosebumps
crawling up them like a swarm of hungry insects. It hit
her torso next, and she clenched her teeth together, forcing
herself to stay still – she didn't want the others to know how
scared she was. She took deep breaths through her nose as
she listened to them counting, mouthing along for effect.

"Fifteen. Sixteen. Seventeen."

Mei rubbed her knuckles as Ellie fought the urge
to allow her teeth to chatter together. The swarm had
reached her scalp now, and she could almost feel hundreds

of tiny legs scuttling across her hairline. The thought set off a wave of shudders. Ellie tried to fight them as another gust of wind hit the group, this one so cold Toni hissed in displeasure and Hugo visibly shook next to her.

"Eighteen," Ellie tried to join in again, but her jaw had a mind of its own, her bottom lip trembling furiously. "Nineteen." She tightened every muscle in her body in an effort to stop shaking, forcing her arms and legs ramrod straight. "T-twenty." She tried.

"Almost there," Callum said quickly, his words running together as he made eye contact with Mei. "Do twenty-two on my nod. Twenty-one."

Mei watched him closely. Ellie couldn't remember how to breathe. Callum took a visibly deep breath, eyes firmly on his watch, waiting for midnight.

It beeped.

"Twenty-two." Mei knocked in a way that Ellie assumed must have taken every ounce of strength, but the boom quickly faded to an echo.

Silence.

"Blow out the candle," Toni hissed. Mei quickly followed the instruction, and the room was plunged into darkness for a second, purple spots appearing in Ellie's vision. A match hissed and, slowly, a flame started to flicker in the red wax once more. Ellie rubbed her arms, noticing that the air had returned to its previous warm temperature.

"Now we light our individual candles." Mei's voice shook as she held the wick of a large, church style candle to the little red tea light. It hissed and spat but eventually the flame doubled, and she stood upright, placing it inside a holder that was surrounded by a glass cylinder with an open top. "You next, Callum."

"What's that?" Toni asked, her eyes narrowed as she pointed at Mei's candle. "You never told us to bring one of those."

"I found it at home and thought it would be useful. It's a hurricane lamp. The glass stops the flame from getting blown out, but the open top means it still gets enough oxygen to stay lit."

"Clever." Ellie smiled at her, wishing she'd thought of that herself. She'd just thrown in whatever she could find in the emergency drawer at home.

"Cheat," she heard Toni hiss.

Ellie moved along the line, waiting for her turn. Hugo managed to light his candle eventually, after what seemed like a hundred tries with a shaking hand. She lit hers quickly, used to the process. She stared into the pool of molten red wax, felt the urge to press her finger into it, like she did when she was a kid. The wax was red as blood in the low light.

She hoped it wasn't any kind of premonition.

Reece and Toni lit theirs together, the latter too impatient to wait any longer. Ellie was surprised she'd let anyone go first. Maybe the sassy goth-girl thing was all an act. Maybe she was as scared as the rest of them.

"Do you think it worked?" Ellie whispered. They were back in the semi-circle around the door, all looking at their names.

"Only one way to—" Mei was cut off mid-sentence as the red candle went out.

01/07/2022   16:34

FrenchBanana: Do you actually think he *is* real? That this whole "ritual" will really summon some kind of entity?

Donttalktome12: Maybe. Probably not, I guess, but the story has to come from somewhere, right?

User3678: It *did* come from somewhere – the depths of the internet. It's a creepy pasta.

CreepyTeepee: Yeah, but so was Slenderman.

Donttalktome12: Fair point.

HotDog45: What's Slenderman?

FrenchBanana: What?

YeahBoi_121: Seriously? Even I know what that is.

User3678: Dude, how did you even end up on this forum???

HotDog45: I like spooky stuff, just not that creepy pasta stuff. It's stupid, just playground stories.

FrenchBanana: Yeah, but everything is just some kind of story, isn't it? At least until you've experienced it first-hand.

CreepyTeepee: Then you're just someone else telling the story.

YeahBoi_121: Very poetic @CreepyTeepee.

User3678: *Vom noises*

HotDog45: No one gonna tell me then?

FrenchBanana: Give me a second.

16:40

FrenchBanana: So, a few years ago there were these three girls in America. All best mates, around thirteen years old. Two of them – can't remember names but I'll link an article – were obsessed with Slenderman. He's meant to be this scary, tall figure who lives in the woods and punishes children or something. He wears a black suit, has no face and has these tentacles that come out of his back. Very incognito, right? Well, the two girls decided that if they killed their other best friend then Slenderman would reward them and they could go and live in his mansion with all the other creepy pasta monsters. They had convinced themselves that if they didn't kill her, Slenderman would come and hurt them and their families – or so they said, anyway.

16:41

CreepyTeepee: I remember this, I think. My mum put a block on the internet after it happened.

HotDog45: No way @*FrenchBanana*! So did they do it?

FrenchBanana: Yeah. They attacked her, but she didn't die. They got caught in the woods later that day, looking for the creepy mansion. They really believed it.

User3678: How did they even come up with the idea? Like, what would you do if your bestie suggested offing someone?

FrenchBanana: Well, *I'd* call the police, but there's a whole psychological theory about two people coming together to do something like this. *Folie a deux* it's called.

YeahBoi_121: It's French. *Folie a deux* is something like "the madness of two"?

FrenchBanana: Yeah, that's right. It's when two people share the same disturbing ideas. A Bonnie and Clyde type of thing.

FrenchBanana: BTW I'm *not* explaining who Bonnie and Clyde are. Wikipedia is your friend here.

HotDog45: Lol, beat me to it *@FrenchBanana*.

YeahBoi_121: That is hideous, isn't it? To do that to their friend too. How could you?

User3678: Cold-blooded bitches.

FrenchBanana: Yeah. I think they're in prison now. Here's a link: www.worldnews.com/slendermanstabbings

16:46

HotDog45: Dude, that is effed up. So, you think the Midnight Man is the same kind of story? Just a creepy pasta?

FrenchBanana: Probably.

User3678: I read it was based on an ancient Pagan ritual, though. They used it to punish wrongdoers back in the day.

Donttalktome12: That in itself sounds very Slenderman, no?

FrenchBanana: Yeah, I guess so.

Donttalktome12: It does. But creepy pasta literally means copy and paste. That's what those stories are, after all, just things that have been copied and pasted over and over again, but with little tweaks each time. Like that game, Telephone. You whisper in someone's ear, then they whisper it to another person and by the end of the game the final message only vaguely sounds like the original.

CreepyTeepee: So, we don't think it's real?

FrenchBanana: I don't.

Donttalktome12: Same.

CreepyTeepee: I dunno… I read that Pagan ritual thing too. Like, Druid stuff. And get this – after someone had been "dealt with" by the Midnight Man, other people would use the dead person's blood. They carved their own names into stones using the runic alphabet and painted the blood on to them. Something about the wrongdoer's blood kept the Midnight Man away, like a protection charm or something.

FrenchBanana: Cool. I didn't see that one. So some sources say the game has been around for thousands of years?

CreepyTeepee: If not longer.

User3678: But why would anyone *want* to play? If it was a punishment?

HotDog45: Aha! The million-pound question.

YeahBoi_121: Because one of our best – and worst – traits as human beings is curiosity. We can't help ourselves.

Donttalktome12: ^What they said.

FrenchBanana: Well, I *am* curious. I mean, I guess we all are, right? Or we wouldn't even be on this site.

CreepyTeepee: Right.

16:51

HotDog45: So, what time are we meeting tomorrow?

MEI

Mei swallowed the scream that wanted to claw its way free from her throat. She knew for a fact she hadn't blown that candle out.

"Maybe it just burnt out," Ellie answered the unspoken question. Her voice sounded wobbly, as though her teeth were chattering, and Mei took some comfort in that. She wasn't the only one who was terrified.

"Maybe," Mei replied, the lack of confidence clear in her voice. It hadn't burnt out on its own, she knew it hadn't. They had hundreds of those tea lights at home; they used them for Mum's little ancestral prayer altar in the hallway. They should last for a few hours, not less than five minutes.

"We don't need it any more, do we? All our candles are lit. So, who wants to do the honours?" Hugo asked, nodding to the door. His voice was booming, even though he spoke quietly. "Mei? You probably should. Open the door, finish the ritual and all that."

"I guess." God, could she sound more non-committal? She was the one who had put herself in charge of this whole escapade. "Sure you have everything?" Everyone mumbled their agreement. Hugo and Reece both patted deep pockets and Callum held up a battered black rucksack. The other girls had bags over their shoulders, Ellie's a heavy looking tote and Toni's a miniature backpack which couldn't have much of anything in it. "All right then." Mei collected her satchel and ducked her head under the strap so it lay securely across her chest like a seatbelt. She straightened it out and pushed the bulk of the bag behind her, taking a deep, shaking breath.

She reached one hand forward, carefully balancing her candle in the other. The smooth, round brass handle was cool to the touch and a tremor ran from her index finger straight up to her shoulders, forcing them to spasm.

"What's wrong?" Toni hissed. That girl always sounded impatient.

"Nothing." Mei forced confidence into her voice and twisted the doorknob, ignoring the shooting sensation. "Here we go."

She wasn't sure what she expected, but the prefab

corridor was not it. Mei stepped in, realizing just how dark it was without the lighting track overhead switched on. A little light filtered through the scratched safety glass of the temporary windows, so between those and the candle, she could just about make out where she was going. It was fairly narrow in there, just wide enough for two kids to squeeze past, or maybe one child and an adult. The same scratchy green carpet covered the floor, and she continued forward, noting a slight decline as the corridor led towards the main building.

"It's already open. I went around and unlocked everything before," Callum said, catching up with her. "Good job back there, by the way."

Mei smiled, but even she knew that it didn't reach her eyes. "Thanks." He was nice. Kind. She should stick with him. She gestured at the next door, this one far older and more impressive than the flimsy door they'd performed the ritual at. "After you. I've had enough of going first for a bit."

"No worries." Callum grabbed the handle, looking much more at ease than Mei had felt, and pushed the door inwards.

Mei followed him past a stairwell and down a short corridor before emerging into an airy, open space. She craned her neck back carefully, not giving her candle a chance to catch a breeze despite the glass encircling it. Above them was an elaborately corniced ceiling, the patterns highlighted by the floor to ceiling windows on the upper level. An old stone staircase swept down to meet them in the entrance hall.

"Whoa."

The rest of the group piled in behind her.

"Dude, this place is *posh*," Reece said in an exaggerated whisper.

"Why are you whispering?" Toni's voice rasped through the stagnant air.

The school had only been closed for one day, but it already felt too still. Places like this should be full of noise. Of life.

"I dunno," Reece said, his smile crooked. He looked like one of those guys who didn't take anything seriously, and Mei was jealous of and frustrated by him all at once. She knew she should loosen up a little bit, it was only a stupid game after all, but she was so used to being serious all the time. Working hard, getting good grades. Being a stickler for the rules was something that was expected of her.

What her parents did *not* expect her to do was to stuff the bed with pillows (and Mr Fluff) before climbing out of her window and running off to break into a primary school.

"So, what now?" Mei watched with slight envy as Ellie spoke. She was confident and pretty and the boys had clearly noticed her too. Hugo in particular was already following her around like a puppy dog. She looked down at her own baggy Pikachu T-shirt and folded an arm across her flat chest.

"We play," Mei said simply. "We follow the rules and we meet back in the hut at three thirty-three a.m. No sooner, no later. We have to keep moving, keep our candles lit and avoid the Midnight Man."

"And if our candles go out?" Hugo asked. His hand was wrapped around a tall, taupe-coloured candle so tightly that his knuckles shone white in the gloom. It looked like he'd liberated it from one of those ridiculously long dining tables you see in movies about rich people.

"That means he's nearby," Mei said. She almost expected someone to giggle, or for Toni to at least roll her eyes, but the atmosphere had suddenly turned sombre. Funereal, almost. "You have to relight it in ten seconds or…" She swallowed as Callum drew a finger across his throat. "Yeah – or that. If you can't, that's what the salt is for. Make a circle around yourself and stay there until the game is over. No matter what happens."

"Do we have to hold this the whole time?" Toni nodded to her own candle. It was in a glass jar and the faint smell of jasmine and fresh linen sheets drifted over from it. "What if I need to go to the loo or something?"

"I don't think so." Mei chose her words carefully. She didn't want to be responsible for everybody if this all went belly-up. "It just says it needs to be with you. So, I guess as long as it's close by you don't need to be physically holding it all of the time. I'll be holding mine, though."

"OK," Toni said. That was it: no argument, no smart comment.

"OK," Mei repeated.

The group stared at each other in their pools of candlelight. It was like something out of a bad horror movie. Mei suddenly really missed her own bed – and Mr Fluff.

"So," Callum's faux-cheerful voice broke the silence. "Who wants a tour?"

01/07/2022   16:52

Donttalktome12: Eleven thirty tomorrow night, then? No point in meeting any earlier.

FrenchBanana: Yeah, that's fine with me.

YeahBoi_121: Can we circle back to the rules for a sec? I know *what* we need, but *why* do we need it? What does the salt do?

CreepyTeepee: Salt is a protective element.

User3678: Salt is for protection.

FrenchBanana: Yay for people doing research!

YeahBoi_121: Protection how?

FrenchBanana: Well, salt protects you from spirits in lots of different cultures. Praying and stuff can help too, I think. Any kind of prayer should work; I don't think it has to be all bibles and crosses like in every white Western horror movie ever made. But salt seems to be a specific part of The Midnight Game.

HotDog45: So – say my candle goes out and I can't relight it. Do I just sit on the floor and draw a circle around myself with the salt? Why not just do that at the start? I could just have a nap until it's all over.

FrenchBanana: No. And also – no.

CreepyTeepee: You can't fall asleep! It's in the rules.

HotDog45: Rules, schmules. I live to break the rules.

User3678: Oh God.

YeahBoi_121: @*HotDog45* is kind of right, though? Not the sleeping bit, but you could theoretically wait it out in your circle?

FrenchBanana: Yesssss, I guess…

YeahBoi_121: But?

Donttalktome12: But you're more vulnerable. When you stay in one spot, even with the salt around you, he knows where you are. The Midnight Man *really* doesn't play by the rules. He will try to lure you out of your safe space and then you've had it.

HotDog45: How does he do that, though?

CreepyTeepee: He plays tricks. He will make you hear things, see things…

User3678: Some say when he tastes your blood, he can also taste your greatest fears. Your biggest secrets.

Donttalktome12: Or it could be the fact that everyone has to write their secrets down and he could, you know, read them…

User3678: OK, yes, it could be that too.

FrenchBanana: That's why you have to keep it safe! Anyway, no matter how he finds out, he will try every dirty trick in the book to get you to leave that circle. Either that or he'll just drive you slowly insane.

YeahBoi_121: Like that girl in the article.

FrenchBanana: Yeah. Maybe.

Donttalktome12: You convinced yet, @HotDog45? It's definitely better to keep moving.

HotDog45: So we just walk around for three and a half hours? Won't that be boring?

FrenchBanana: God, I hope so.

CALLUM

"Where first?" Toni asked. Callum narrowed his eyes to get a better look at her as she spoke. She acted as though she was unshakable, but she looked so young in the candlelight. They all did really. Especially Mei.

"Right here." Callum took long strides to the centre of the foyer, one hand cupped, watching his flickering candle with each step. He stopped and rested his free hand on the bottom of a heavy wooden banister. It curved up a twisting set of stairs towards the looming stone ceiling, the polished wood cool on his sweaty palm. A huge wooden crucifix hung over them, thin chains holding its weight on the wall. Callum shuddered. The gory depiction of Christ on the cross had always made him uncomfortable, and this one seemed particularly graphic, especially for a school. "There are only two floors, but everything centres around this staircase. Even if you end up walking in circles, you should always come back to this. We're right in the middle of the building here. So, if you do get lost, just keep going until you hit these stairs. The door to the hut is right down there." He pointed at the hallway they'd just emerged from, hoping he was keeping this simple. "Come on, let's go right first."

Callum took long, steady steps as he ducked into a long corridor. He glanced over his shoulder, careful to keep the candle still while making sure the rest of the group were actually behind him. He hid a sigh of relief when he saw that they were. They followed him slowly, every pair of eyes fixed on their own candle flame. This would be slow going; they'd be lucky if they got around once in the time they had. He saw Ellie cup a hand around her flame and smile at Hugo, who immediately copied her. Callum did the same.

"These are the music rooms," he tipped his head to the left. "See how small they are? This building used to be an old law court and those rooms were cells. There's a blocked-up staircase somewhere that the criminals would have walked up to see the judge in the main hall."

"That's pretty cool," Reece said, sticking his head through the doorway. "Bit of a creepy place to learn the recorder, though."

"Oh, God." Ellie let out a bark of a laugh that Callum didn't expect from her. "Recorder flashbacks." She winced as though she could hear the shrill sound. "Trauma."

"Right? I used to dread recorder lessons. All that spit." Toni snorted a laugh. Callum smiled as he carried on down the corridor, gently pushing open a door and finding the doorstop with his foot. He pushed the heavy rubber wedge under the bottom of the door to prop it open. Maybe they could be nice to each other for a couple of hours after all.

"This is one of the classrooms," he said, walking into the room as the others clustered together at the doorway. It was much nicer than the hut: the displays on the walls were bright and colourful even in their dark surroundings. Thick, blue plastic chairs stood on top of rectangular tables that were grouped together around the room. Callum could almost see the little boys and girls who worked, argued and played in this room day after day. Guilt gnawed at him, but he pushed it away. It was fine. Mum would never find out. "They're all pretty similar, but I thought if we wedged the doors open, we will be able to wander in and out. It gives us a lot more space to walk around in."

"Good idea." Mei smiled at him, her shoulders a little more relaxed than they had been. "Where are we looking next?"

Callum followed the group out and resumed his place as tour guide. He gestured to the other side of the corridor and Hugo stepped forward, pushing the door open and wedging it as Callum had done with the last one. Good, this was starting to look like teamwork.

"It's another classroom. Looks a bit bigger, though," Hugo told them.

"Yeah, the ones at the front of the building are. There are two classrooms on this corridor."

"What's in there, then? A cupboard or something?" Toni pointed down the hall, her chipped black nail almost resting on Callum's shoulder. They were halfway down the corridor, so he picked up as much speed as he could and walked towards it. He held his candle up to the small brass plaque on the door.

Library.

"A library!" Mei almost squealed the word, and a ripple of nervous laughter flowed from one person to the next as her voice echoed around the empty space. "Oops, sorry." She winced. "I just really like books."

"Me too," Ellie said kindly. "Can we go in with our candles? Or would it be too dangerous?"

"Nah, I'm sure we'll be OK." Callum pushed the door open and beckoned them in. "This bit is an extension. They got funding from ... well, somewhere, to build it all brand new. It's really nice."

Mei wasted no time in crossing the threshold, and Callum hung back by the door, narrowing his eyes to search for the doorstop. He knew there should be one somewhere around here, he'd kicked them out while helping to lock up often enough. Finally, with a little help from the streetlight outside streaming in through the library windows, he spotted the heavy rubber wedge and nudged it under the door, maintaining the careful balancing act that meant keeping his flame alive.

"I never had a library like this at my primary school," Toni whispered as Callum turned around to rejoin the group. Her face had softened a little, and Callum could see a hint of wonder beneath the heavy make-up. "We just had a shelf in the classroom with some ratty old books on it. They were so ancient that the covers had all torn off; no one was interested in them at all."

Callum looked at the room through fresh eyes. It was a nice space, ringed by walls lined with shelf after shelf of books in all sizes. Bright banners advertised the different sections and at the very front there was an alcove that looked out on to the street, complete with a seating area and floor-to-ceiling picture window, though the view was unfortunately partly obscured by the prefab corridor that led back to the hut. A thick rug covered the school-issue carpet and was dotted with beanbags that looked as though they were well-used.

"We had a library, but it wasn't like this either," Mei tried to make conversation. "Just a few shelves and some colour-coded stickers for the different reading levels out in the play area. I used to love these, though." She carefully prised a slim volume from the shelf in front of her and held it up for Toni and Callum to see. The cover was battered, the corners soft and dog-eared and the title dripped from the page, surrounded by a sea of bubbling green slime. "My parents would never let me read them at home, so I used to keep them in my tray and read under the desk whenever I had finished my work. I got caught so many times, but my teacher said she was the same when she was a kid and let me carry on. I think they're what started my love of the supernatural."

"That's cool." Toni smiled for a split second before putting her face back together. "If you're a total geek, I guess."

Callum winced as Mei flushed and Toni sauntered away. "Ignore her," he said, "she's just a mean girl. Don't let her issues rub off on you."

"OK." Mei sniffed and Callum shrank back under her watery, slightly adoring gaze. "Thank you."

"Er, no problem." He looked over the top of her head to see Hugo and Ellie huddled in a corner. They were whispering near a small table that held an ancient desktop computer. Reece stood near them, pretending to browse the titles on the Religious Education shelf, but he was clearly staring at Ellie's tanned legs instead. "Hey," Callum called over to them quietly, "what are you guys doing?"

"Nothing." Hugo choked on the word, coughing and spluttering as Ellie patted him delicately on the back with her free hand. The sweet, sharp smell of alcohol drifted across the room.

"You have booze?" Toni asked, her eyebrows hiked in amusement. "Can you even have alcohol in the game?"

"Doesn't say you can't, does it?" Reece piped up, reluctantly returning his gaze to eye-level. "Share the love, mate." He held a confident hand out for the flask, but Hugo hesitated. "Come on, I could do with a shot to relieve the boredom."

"There's not that much in it," Hugo said apologetically, sliding a palm-sized silver hipflask from his back pocket. It was banded with soft, tan leather and Callum guessed there was a monogram stamped somewhere. He hid a smile. Of *course* Hugo carried a personalized hipflask. "I do reckon there's enough for a good swig each, if you don't mind sharing?"

"I'm game." Toni grinned in the gloom, her teeth shining. *Like a great white shark*, Callum thought.

"Yeah, why not?" Ellie shrugged, though Callum felt pretty sure she'd already had a sip.

"Whatever." Callum said as the group slowly fell into a circle. He glanced down at Mei. "Just pretend if you want," he whispered to her, but she shook her head, eyes gleaming.

"No, I'm curious. I want to."

"OK, up to you."

"Here you go, pal." Hugo flipped the top of the flask

open with a brawny thumb and gamely handed it straight to Reece. "It's a Scotch. Single malt, barrel aged…"

"It's a what?" Reece took the flask with his free hand and sniffed gingerly. "Wow, that's like paint stripper."

"No, it's Scottish whisky. A good year too." He recited the words like poetry: "It will warm your bones against the chill of the evening."

"It'll make you chunder," Toni whispered, and a nervous giggle rippled around the group.

"Nah, I've got a lead stomach." Reece held the flask aloft. "Cheers!" He took a swig from the flask and immediately made a sucking noise with his teeth. "Oh, that's spicy," he choked out.

"Spicy?" Mei laughed as she took the flask from him, her hand shaking slightly. "Er, bottoms up?" She gently lifted the flask, the metal clinking on the frame of her glasses. "Urgh, the smell is so strong."

"Hold your nose," Ellie suggested, pinching a thumb and forefinger over her own to show Mei what she meant. "You'll taste it less that way too."

"OK." Mei copied the gesture, shutting the air off from each nostril. She lifted the flask to her lips and sipped gingerly. "Hey, that wasn't too…" As soon as she removed the fingers from her nose she made a retching sound. "Oh my god, that's disgusting." Her small body convulsed as she fought to keep it down, and Callum worried for a second that she would be sick in front of everyone – or that she would drop her candle.

"You OK?" he whispered.

"Get this away from me." She groaned, thrusting the open flask at him. For a second, everything wobbled and he thought he would either drop it or the candle, but he recovered both. A small bead of sweat trickled from the back of his hairline down past his hood and soaked into the collar of his T-shirt. That was close.

"Good one, Mei." Reece clapped his free hand on his leg in appreciation as Mei gave him a shaky grin. Callum held up the flask in a salute before lifting it to his lips. He pressed them together tightly, hoping the darkness was covering him, that it didn't look to obvious he wasn't actually drinking.

"Nice one." Toni took the flask and drank casually, as though she'd done it a thousand times, only pausing to grit her teeth before passing the Scotch on to Ellie. She sniffed it and wrinkled her nose, making her look like a cute little bunny. She took a swig and made an exaggerated face, though to Callum she looked almost as well practised as Toni did.

"Wow." Ellie coughed a little before handing the flask back to Hugo. "That's definitely an … acquired taste."

"It's my father's stash," Hugo said, shaking the flask. One final shot sloshed around inside and he held it up. "It cost an absolute fortune. The man has great taste." He downed the rest of the Scotch and let out a rasp of air.

"Shame he's an utter twat."

"Yes, mate!" Reece shouted and slapped his thigh again.

Another ripple of laughter caught the group as Callum licked his lips, tasting the bitter sting of the alcohol that lingered there as his eyes focused on the large picture window that should have looked out on to the street.

It was dark outside, made even more so by the corridor that ran past, so the group with their flickering candles were reflected back in the window. Not quite a mirror image, but the shade of a reflection. He watched, mesmerized, their shadows shifting and twisting around in the glass as the group split up. Callum scrutinized their shadows as they drifted, one in particular seeming to loom large over the doorway. It grew in the reflection and a cold breeze shot through the room, so cold it penetrated straight through the fibres of his jumper. He cupped his candle automatically and turned around to see the others do the same. He glanced around the room, counting heads.

No one was near the door.

Slowly he turned back to the window, just in time to see the shadow slide up and across the ceiling. "Er, shall we get out of here, guys? Carry on with the tour?"

A murmur of agreement led them towards the door. He must have imagined it – everyone else was calm, focused on their candles.

"Wait!" Toni screamed, breaking the silence.

"What is it?" Callum tried to keep the edge from his voice and failed, his eyes darting around. He just wanted to get out of there.

"My candle has gone out."

01/07/2022   17:14

YeahBoi_121: When you say *"he can taste your worst fear"*, what do you mean exactly?

FrenchBanana: Well, like @Donttalktome12 said, he could just get the paper away from you and read it, but the original legend goes that The Midnight Man would taste the blood of the wrongdoer and he would then know everything about them. I suppose in Pagan times people would only be able to write their name, if they could even do that. So instead, it happened the gory way and he found out the secrets they harboured, the reason they were there, etc. Like a sick sort of telepathy, I guess.

Donttalktome12: He would know everything?

CreepyTeepee: *Everything.* Especially anything that you were ashamed of or hiding. It was a punishment, remember? The Midnight Man would know what the person had done wrong by tasting their blood and finding out everything about them. The writing bit seems to be a more modern addition.

Donttalktome12: Damn.

User3678: What if you have nothing to hide? Like, you've never done anything wrong. Some of us are perfect angels…

CreepyTeepee: Lol.

CreepyTeepee: Seriously? I dunno. I'd have thought that all of us have done something bad at some point, even if we didn't mean it.

17:16

CreepyTeepee: Right?

17:18

HotDog45: Say you haven't. Will he just leave you alone?

FrenchBanana: I doubt it. *You* summon *him*. So I think he kind of assumes you've done something wrong. He's just there for the game.

HotDog45: World's most jacked up game of hide and seek. I love it.

FrenchBanana: I suppose it is. And The Midnight Man will just keep chasing you until it's over…

CreepyTeepee: And hopefully you survive.

User3678: I refer you back to my earlier statement: why would anyone want to play?

YeahBoi_121: Not chickening out on us, are you, @User3678?

User3678: Hell no. I just like to have some kind of insight into the motives of my enemy, that's all.

HotDog45: OK – say he gets you. Finds out your big, bad wrongdoing. What then? He spanks you and makes you say sorry to Daddy?

FrenchBanana: Ewwwwww. Not quite.

CreepyTeepee: Lol, no.

YeahBoi_121: What happens then?

FrenchBanana: Well, firstly, it only happens if everything so far has gone wrong, because he can only "get" you if you don't follow the rules.

CreepyTeepee: Then he subjects you to your greatest fear.

TONI

"No, no, no! Help me!" Toni's hand shook far more violently than she would have liked. A thin tendril of smoke danced away from the faintly glowing wick and a line of molten wax dripped over the softened edge of the candle, directly on to the tender skin between her thumb and forefinger. "Ouch!" She swapped hands and shook out her injured one.

Behind her, someone started counting.

"Ten…"

"Where are your matches?" Toni looked up to see the bimbo standing in front of her. "Do you need to borrow mine?"

"I have some." Toni forced her sore hand into the pocket

99

of her leather jacket and pulled out a small matchbox. The matches rattled as she pushed the little drawer out with one finger. "These are such a pain in the arse."

"Seven…"

"I think that's the point. Here." The bimbo – Ellie, Toni begrudgingly corrected herself – took the candle from her, leaving both of Toni's hands free to strike a match. She gritted her teeth, forced her hand to stop shaking, and scraped the little wooden stick until there was a sharp hiss and crackle as the match caught. Her nostrils flared with the smell of sulphur as she guided it over towards the blackened wick.

"Five…"

"It's so cold." Mei's voice was so small Toni barely heard her, but it *was* freezing, even with her jacket and tights on. The back of Toni's neck started to prickle as the hairs there stood straight up, cold air drifting through them. The feeling was a warning as old as time, something primal.

Danger.

"Hurry," Ellie whispered, her own hand shivering. Toni could see the gooseflesh on her arms and willed the candle to catch.

Another gust of wind blew through the room, taking the flame with it. "No!" Toni glared at the dead match in disbelief.

"Three…"

Ellie's candle was still alight, the gust of wind blocked

by her body. "Just light it off yours," Toni ordered, hoping she didn't sound like she was pleading with her.

"She can't," Callum chimed in. He was stood with Mei, who was consulting her watch as she counted. "It's against the rules. You have to re-light it with a match, not from another candle."

"Two…"

"Come on! Toni, Toni! Look at me." The sharp edge in Ellie's voice roused her back to attention. "You've got this. Come on, just one more."

Toni snapped into focus. She dropped the spent match, pulled another and struck it off the side in one fluid motion. This time she cupped her shaking hand as the sulphur flared and closed her palm around the candle and flame, willing it to catch. Another gust of wind rocked the room.

"One."

The room itself seemed to hold its breath. Toni stared at her hands, too scared to pull them away in case the candle wasn't lit. Seconds passed and the wind died down before she shakily unwrapped them, revealing the flame that had been kindled there.

"Good job." Ellie smiled, holding the candle out to her. Ugh, she was so *nice*.

"Naturally." Toni took it and pushed the box of matches back into her pocket. She patted it and pulled the zip up carefully. She didn't want to lose those, did she?

"That was quite intense." Hugo said, clearly trying for humour, but it fell flat. Even Reece looked shook.

"Where did that wind come from, though?" Mei whispered.

Toni straightened herself out and rearranged her face into a snarl. "Outside, obviously. There must be air vents in each room."

"But I thought…" Callum trailed off, glancing at the door.

"You thought what?" Toni snapped.

"Oh, nothing."

"No, come on. Spit it out," she demanded. The others whipped their heads between her and the gangly boy like they were watching a tennis match.

"I thought I saw something," he croaked.

"Really?" Mei asked, her eyes so wide it looked painful.

"Yeah." Callum cleared his throat, rubbing the back of his neck with his free hand. "In the reflection on the window."

"What was it?" Ellie asked, her voice shaking slightly. She was nice, maybe, but she clearly lacked backbone. Typical.

"Just … shadows," he admitted. "It was probably nothing, I mean our candles are casting all sorts of shapes on to the walls." He gestured to their dancing shadow selves. They were wild things who clambered over books and grazed the ceiling with long, spindly limbs. Toni blinked quickly to rid herself of the image.

"It was probably nothing," Callum said finally.

"Of course it was nothing," Toni spat, forcing her hands to stop shaking as she glared pointedly at him. "Let's keep moving, shall we?" Her words hung in the air for a second, and she wondered if he'd argue back, say it was her own fault they were still there.

"Yeah, let's go. Upstairs next?" Callum gestured for the others to follow, and Toni hung back, waiting until she was the last one in line, even though on the inside she was dying to push her way to the front. They left the library and went through a swinging door to the left, which led to a fire exit door and a stairwell.

"Is it too late to leave?" Hugo eyed the metal bar across the fire door that led to freedom, with something like regret. Toni studied him as the others followed Callum up the stairs.

"You know it is," Toni cooed, trying to copy Ellie's soft voice. "Remember the rules? *'Don't go outside.'*"

"I know, I know. That was just a bit…"

"Intense?" she interrupted, watching Ellie climb the stairs in front of her. Girl must do her squats; she was in great shape. No wonder the boys were drooling over her. It almost made Toni want to exercise. Almost. "Scary?"

"No, of course not. More – ah – unexpected." Hugo tripped over his words and Toni wondered how much effort it was taking him to maintain his calm and collected facade. His hand visibly trembled as they followed the others on to the stairs. Toni stepped up behind him, guarding her candle with her whole upper body.

This staircase wasn't as grand as the one in the main entrance hall, far from it, actually. Where that one was crafted from limestone and hand-carved wood, this was all metal railings and rough carpet. Despite the latter detail, every step echoed. It was the kind of stairwell you'd find in a multistorey car park.

The kind you walked through quickly.

Toni was definitely regretting being at the back of the line.

She focused on the staircase to distract herself. It was designed to be crammed into a small space – a few steps up, followed by a turn in the landing and another few steps to the top. The strange, candlelit procession climbed them at a snail's pace and by the time Toni was on the third step Callum was almost at the top. She stayed close behind Hugo as she watched the others climb higher, each slowly making progress, one hand wrapped around their flame while the other held the candle. Nobody wanted to sacrifice their light after what had just happened in the library, so the railing stayed untouched as they felt for each step in the dark. Toni imagined what would happen if Callum lost his footing. They'd go down like dominoes, flames catching on each other as they tumbled down in one big fiery ball.

She let Hugo take a couple of steps ahead of her before moving again.

"Come on through." She reached the top of the

drab stairwell to be greeted by Callum holding open an identical swinging door to the one downstairs. Everyone else was in the corridor already, waiting in silence. She passed him, careful not to let the draught catch her flame, and looked both ways.

"Looks just the same as downstairs," she muttered.

"It is." Callum was pushing wedges into doors again. "Apart from that this is a cupboard – not the library. That was a single-storey extension." He pushed open doors exactly where they had been downstairs, revealing two more large window-lined classrooms as they followed him down the corridor.

Toni trailed behind, peeking into the rooms. The last one seemed to be an art or maybe design tech room. There was never anything like that when she was at primary school; if you were lucky you got to do some gluing at your table and that was about it. If you were even more lucky, you'd have time to paint your hand with the PVA and let it dry, before trying to peel it off in one huge sheet. God, that had been satisfying. From what she could see in here there were drying racks for paintings, a line of pegs on the wall hung with clay-smeared aprons and several storage towers filled with blue plastic drawers. These were labelled with their contents, laminated paper printed in Comic Sans declaring "*Junior hacksaws*" or "*Paper straws*".

"So, when we get to here, do you know where you are?" Toni snapped back to the present, following Callum's voice through a set of double glass doors. She walked through the one that Callum had propped open, stopped and glanced around. They appeared to be back in the main hall, only the staircase here was leading down, not up.

"Oh, yeah. Nice one, that was easy," Reece said. He was rummaging in the pocket of his huge tracksuit bottoms with one hand, obviously struggling to do that and hold his candle.

"What on earth are you looking for?" Mei asked, pushing her glasses up with her free hand.

"Ahhhh!" Reece called in triumph, retrieving a crinkling cellophane bag. "I need a sugar boost. Anyone want some sweets?"

"Er, no thanks." Toni looked at the bag in disgust. "I'm not really in the mood for warm-crotch jellies. Thanks, though."

"Your loss, sweetheart," he crowed, holding the bag between his knees while he used his free hand to find the little notch in the seal and tear it open. A couple of tiny gelatine bears made a leap for freedom, their colours catching in the candlelight as they fell, but Reece saved the rest of the bag. Despite her snide comment, Toni's mouth started to water.

"Are they veggie?" Callum asked, eyeing the mixture of gummy hearts and rings.

"Not a scooby." Reece shrugged. "Here." He grabbed a fistful and passed the bag to Callum, who held his candle up to the ingredients.

"Yessss, you legend," he hissed, taking a handful. "Anyone else?"

"Maybe." Ellie had dropped her bag to the floor and was currently crouching down, candle-arm held away from her as the other hand felt around inside it. Toni watched her curiously. What did she have in there? "I need to check my blood sugar." She said it apologetically. "My phone normally lets me know if my blood sugars are high or low, but I don't have it with me. I'm getting a bit of a headache and it's been a while since I've eaten, so … ah, here." She pulled out a slim, black wallet and put the bag back on her shoulder. "It won't take me long to check my levels, but I will need to stay still for a few minutes. You guys carry on the tour, though, I can catch up."

"No!" Mei's voice was strained as Toni turned to look at her. "No," she repeated, more firmly this time. "We need to stick together. It's not even one o'clock yet; we have hours to go."

"She's right," Toni drawled, earning herself surprised looks. "What? I might not be shaking in my Docs, but I don't want to be on my own in this creepy ass place. There's a box labelled "*Junior hacksaws*" in that room."

"Oh, I hated those," Mei groaned. "I was so bad at manoeuvring them, the handle was so awkward, and the blade seemed to have all these teeth. I always worried I'd slip and hack a finger off." She shuddered and Toni hid a smirk.

"Tell you what." Callum turned to face a pair of large wooden doors that had been partially hidden by the darkness. "That's the assembly hall. It's where the trials used to be held in the olden days. We'll go in there so Ellie can check her blood sugar level."

Toni rolled her eyes, but Callum stood up straight and levelled her with a stare. "We will go in there so Ellie can check her bloods because the last thing we need in the next few hours is a medical emergency. Right?" He stared her directly in the eye, waiting for an answer. Brave kid.

"Whatever," she shrugged. "No skin off my nose."

"Good. It's big in there and usually empty. We can keep moving but keep an eye on Ellie too."

"We could put some salt around her to keep her safe?" Hugo suggested, making puppy-dog eyes at the pretty blonde.

"No, don't waste it," Ellie replied. "I can do this with one hand and still hold the candle. I'll be fine."

"Come on, then." Callum pulled the huge wooden door open, the effort showing on his face. It was clearly heavier than the classroom doors. Hugo grabbed the other, muscles straining beneath his polo shirt, and they filtered through into the large hall. Ellie immediately plonked herself down on the floor, unzipping her diabetes bag and removing a finger pricker. The others shuffled around the room until Toni decided to break the silence.

"So," she began, "we know Mei is scared of slicing a finger off. What about the rest of you?"

"What do you mean?" Hugo asked through a mouthful of sweets.

"I mean," Toni said, her eyes twinkling like dying stars, "what's everyone's greatest fear?"

01/07/2022   17:25

HotDog45: Your greatest fear?

FrenchBanana: Yeah. Pretty horrible, right?

HotDog45: But how does the Midnight Man do that? Like, say I hate sharks. Is he going to turn into a shark? What if there's no water? Will he chase me around with a fake fin strapped to his back?

User3678: Well, that would be a sight...

FrenchBanana: No, don't be ridiculous. It's much more subtle than that. He gets inside your head, makes you hallucinate...

CreepyTeepee: I read he makes you feel like you're living in your worst nightmare. Tries to scare you to death.

YeahBoi_121: But what if your greatest fear is something more abstract?

HotDog45: ???

FrenchBanana: You mean something intangible? Like, a feeling?

User3678: *Googles intangible*

FrenchBanana: Means it's real but you can't touch it. Like pride, or sadness. Something like that.

Donttalktome12: You mean like failure? Some people are scared to fail. How would the Midnight Man make you hallucinate that?

FrenchBanana: I really don't know.

CreepyTeepee: Oh God, what about a never-ending exam. Like those dreams when you take a test and you don't know anything on the paper, or your pencil keeps snapping. You just keep failing it over and over again.

YeahBoi_121: That sounds pretty horrendous to me.

HotDog45: I hate real exams, so … yeah. That's grim.

FrenchBanana: *shudders*

HotDog45: Right, hear me out then. What happens if you have a harmless secret, followed by a lame – or at least survivable – worst fear? Is that it? Game over?

YeahBoi_121: Maybe? You burn your paper and then you must win, right?

17:30

YeahBoi_121: Is that how you win?

17:32

FrenchBanana: Nooooo. Not quite.

CreepyTeepee: No. It's pretty bad.

HotDog45: What's pretty bad? How do you not win if you've done all that?

FrenchBanana: Well, for all of this to happen, your candle has blown out and you've left your salt circle. So, unless you can get back to your circle, back to your protection...

YeahBoi_121: WHAT?!

User3678: He slices you open and rips your organs out.

17:35

User3678: While you're still alive.

112

HUGO

Hugo didn't really know what his greatest fears were. Getting caught sneaking Daddy's expensive Scotch, maybe? Or even worse, the keys to his Jag. Or what about that time him and the boys got stuck on Teddy's sailboat on the Menai Strait and ran out of beer? Or, if it was specific to tonight, getting stuck in a room with the scary one, Toni.

That's what he told himself, anyway.

"Come onnnn," Toni drawled. Hugo watched her pace slowly. She exaggerated each movement, planting one foot forward and dragging the toe of her other boot across the floor to catch up. When her feet met, she repeated the whole process, heaving herself around the hall like a shuffling zombie. The sound it made scratched at his ears each time the steel toecap bumped across the ridged carpet.

"I'll tell you mine if you stop doing" – Reece waved a handful of jelly sweets in her direction – "whatever that is. It's freaky enough in here without you going all *Night of the Living Dead* on us."

"OK." She stopped and stood up straight, tilting her head to listen to him. Hugo's eyes flicked to Ellie, who was still on the floor, waving a little strip of card in the air. She was managing to keep hold of the lit candle, just like she'd said. Good. He went back to watching Reece, who was chewing thoughtfully.

"Don't laugh, right?" Reece warned. They had fallen into a circle, pacing one behind the other in order to keep moving, Ellie at the centre of them all. She had been oblivious to everyone watching as she pricked her finger and smeared the resulting blood on to a card that she slotted into a small machine. She must be so used to doing it, but to Hugo it resembled the blood sacrifice they'd made earlier far too closely.

"We won't, promise," Mei chirped, crossing her heart with her free hand. The small girl had perked up since she'd had some of Reece's sugary sweets and she seemed less nervous than before.

"Fine." Reece sighed and dropped a couple more sweets into his mouth. Hugo focused his eyes on the candle flame in his hand, watching it flicker and burn as his feet fell into a rhythm with everyone else. "I don't like cats."

"Cats?!" Ellie's head popped up as she squealed from the middle. "How can you be scared of cats? They're so cute!" She was holding a tiny can of coke and Hugo watched, mesmerized, as she knelt forwards, put it between her knees and popped the tab one handed.

"Yeah, we have two Ragdolls, and they have the most gorgeous, smooshiest faces." Mei laughed, shaking her head. "Cats aren't scary."

"Yes, they are," Reece insisted, frowning at his crowd. "They're shady little creatures with stupid names like *ragdolls*. They hide in your bedroom just to jump on you at four a.m. and give you heart failure. *Then* they have the balls to sit on your chest and lick their own butthole as if nothing has happened. Seriously, they're terrifying. Absolutely ruthless. Plus their tails have a mind of their own. When I was a kid, I woke up with one practically down my oesophagus. My mum lost the plot."

"You … can't … be serious." Toni had slowed right down and was taking deep, sucking breaths in between bouts of laughter. She could barely get the words out whole and Hugo felt a laugh bubble up in his own throat. Before he knew it, they were all howling, Reece included.

"Mate," Callum wheezed, trying to straighten up, "I take it you're definitely a dog person, then?"

"I reckon I'm more of a goldfish person," Reece choked through gulps of air.

Hugo smiled down at Ellie as his laughter subsided. She was still laughing so hard the cola can shook and dark liquid spilled down her forearm. As Hugo watched she looked him in the eye and slowly licked it off, letting her tongue linger on her lips for a second before shooting him a filthy smile and winking slowly at him.

What the hell? He rubbed his eyes with his free hand and looked around the room. Everyone was pacing again; the moment of wild laughter had faded and the faces showed him that people had remembered why they were here. No one seemed to have noticed that Ellie had just turned full sex kitten. When Hugo glanced back at her she was on her feet, putting her rubbish back in her bag. She stepped into line behind him.

"All sorted," she said. "No hypo, but my levels were dipping a bit. That should last me an hour or so before I have to check again." She smiled at him, an open, innocent smile this time, and he tried to return it, but his mouth wouldn't cooperate. "What is it?" She ran her tongue across her teeth, as if checking for something stuck there.

"Nothing," Hugo whispered, avoiding eye contact. Had he imagined it? Was he reading her signals all wrong and his brain was filling in the blanks, like last time?

"What about you, Tinker-hell?" Reece fired at Toni, dragging Hugo back to the present. She shrugged, nonchalant as she strode around the circle.

"Mine's a bit basic bitch, I hate to say." Hugo eyed her

curiously. He didn't for a second think that she'd share her real fear. "Heights. I hate them. My legs go all shaky and my head swims. Get me up something high enough and I think I'd just fall right over."

"They are scary," Ellie's voice was quiet behind Hugo. "Mine's kind of similar to that. Claustrophobia. Cliched, right? But the thought of being buried alive … just, no thank you. It's my ultimate nightmare."

"How are you even worried about that?" Callum asked. "Is it a common fear?"

"I don't know, but once I listened to this podcast and they told a story about how many people were accidentally buried alive in the olden days, before embalming, you know?" Nobody responded. There was only the sound of their footsteps, in sync again now but muffled by the carpet. Ellie carried on explaining and Hugo had to force himself to concentrate. "There was this one woman and someone in her family had a dream that she was still alive, that by burying her they'd made this terrible mistake. They wouldn't shut up about this dream and eventually everyone just had enough. So, they marched down to the graveyard, a big old bunch of them, carrying shovels and picks."

"And was she alive?" Hugo couldn't stop the question from crossing his lips.

"No. She was dead."

"Oh, thank G—"

"But when they looked at her hands, her fingers were torn, bloody stumps and her fingernails had been ripped from their beds. Do you know where they found them?"

"Where?" Mei squeaked. All six of them had drawn closer unconsciously and now everyone was within touching distance. Hugo even thought he could smell a mixture of whisky and strawberry jellies as Mei whispered her question.

"On the inside of the coffin lid. They were embedded there in long, bloody gouge marks."

"But that means…" Hugo started, but Ellie cut him off, focusing her attention on the smaller girl.

"She had been buried alive, after all," Ellie said. Mei's hand shook and Hugo couldn't tear his eyes away from her candle. Ellie continued in oblivion as Mei let out a gasp.

"No," she whispered.

"Yes. She had been buried alive and tried to claw her way out."

"No," Mei croaked, her voice thick with tears. "I didn't mean that. My candle has gone out."

01/07/2022   17:36

HotDog45: Well, that gory little fact proves the game is all fake, doesn't it?

FrenchBanana: What do you mean?

Donttalktome12: They *mean* when is the last time you saw a news report about a bunch of people who had their organs ripped out and thrown around?

User3678: Eviscerated, I think the term is.

FrenchBanana: Ew. Anyway, no one said anything about them being thrown around, did they?

CreepyTeepee: So where do they go? If the Midnight Man eviscerates people, where do their insides go?

YeahBoi_121: Maybe he eats them.

FrenchBanana: JESUS CHRIST, *@YeahBoi_121*.

User3678: Ugh, I feel sick.

HotDog45: Duuuuuuuuuuude, ha! That is *dark*!

YeahBoi_121: Sorry.

17:40

YeahBoi_121: He is, like, a demon, though, isn't he? Don't demons do that kind of thing?

17:42

FrenchBanana: … I *guess* so…

CreepyTeepee: Annnnnnnyway. So, we're really going to do this?

Donttalktome12: Do what?

User3678: Play this bloody game.

Donttalktome12: Oh, you mean break-and-enter a private property, deface a door with human blood, become a massive fire risk and try to avoid an ancient Pagan demon who wants to eat our organs?

HotDog45: That's the one.

Donttalktome12: Coolio. Here's a pin. See you there tomorrow night. 11:30 p.m. at the *latest*.

17:44 @Donttalktome12 dropped a location pin.

📍 *St. Martin's Roman Catholic Primary School, 182 Longmount Road, M29 1BU*

User3678: A Catholic school? Are you serious?

Donttalktome12: Yeah. It's all we've got, unless you have a better idea?

17:46

Donttalktome12: That's what I thought.

FrenchBanana: See you all tomorrow, then! And remember to bring extra candles.

HotDog45: Why?

FrenchBanana: Because if there's one thing we've learned today, it's that we do *not* want our candles to go out.

REECE

"You have to relight it. Quickly." Reece hung back as Callum broke the circle, calmly speaking to Mei as he tried to keep his own candle aflame. The boy seemed to have taken her under his wing, perfect, helpless little duckling that she was.

"I … I don't think I can!" The words left her in sharp, gasping breaths and Reece could almost feel the tears prick at his own eyes. Damn it.

"Here." He joined them, pulling a box of matches from his tracksuit pocket. "Calm down, OK?" He handed the packet to Callum and plucked the hurricane glass off before taking the candle holder from Mei's hand. Someone had started up that godawful countdown behind him again. "We'll be done in no time," he promised, trying his best to sound soothing.

Callum scuffed the match into a flame, and it illuminated the wet cheeks behind Mei's gold-framed glasses. "OK," she sniffed, her eyes not leaving the candle.

"Six…"

"It's not catching," Callum hissed. Reece knew he'd tried to keep his voice low, but Mei was too close not to hear him. "I think the wick is trapped in the wax."

"Nononononono." Mei twisted her hands in the hem of her T-shirt as the countdown went on behind them. The others continued to walk around them, a macabre version of some kids' game. Out of the corner of his eye, Reece saw Ellie trying to search her bag and balance her candle at the same time.

"Four…"

"Dig it out!" Callum's voice was higher than usual, and Reece lowered one knee to the floor, placing the candle flat on the ground. Trying to keep his own candle still, he plunged his fingers into the hot wax.

"Shit!" He pulled scalded fingers out, but as soon as they hit the cooler air, the wax began to solidify on his fingers. He tapped them together, hoping they'd afford him a little protection against the liquid wax and shoved them in again, fishing around the molten pool for the wick.

"Two…"

"It's no good." Reece pulled out a small, blackened lump that smeared across his fingers in the white wax. Mei's eyes were closed now, her palms pressed together as she rocked slowly back and forth, muttering under her breath. "The wick has snapped. It's a dodgy candle. Mei? Mei, listen to me. Do you have a spare candle?"

"Salt," she croaked, opening her eyes and staring straight into Reece's soul.

"One."

"What?" Reece looked back at the rest of the group.

"Salt! Get the salt!" She licked her lips feverishly.

"Time's up." Ellie appeared as if by magic, a large container of table salt in her right hand. "Mei, stay still. You two, move." Reece abandoned Mei's candle and got to his feet again, stepping backwards as Ellie began to pour a thick line of salt around the sobbing girl. The room was deathly silent otherwise. "Come on, you'll be fine." Ellie shot a look at the others, and Reece heard them finally speak up.

"Yes, it's just a game." Hugo sounded more robot than bloke, especially compared to Toni, whose voice was soft for once.

"It's fine, Mei. Just sit in the circle and we'll get your spare candle," she whispered. She crept behind Hugo to stand with Reece and Callum as the four of them tightened into a knot, watching as Ellie continued pouring. A cool draught of wind pushed its way through the open doors of the hall and caught the hem of the long curtains that lined one wall. A ripple passed through the thick material.

"That shouldn't be happening," Callum said, his voice low. He was staring at the curtains too, his eyes so wide that Reece could see the whites all around them. "They're so heavy you have to use a pulley to open them. They have weights sewn into the bottom." Another ripple shivered through the velvet and Reece's eyes grew transfixed on one spot where the shadows seemed to congregate, thick and deep. He pointed.

"Is…" Reece peeled his tongue from the roof of his mouth and tried again. "Is that a man?"

A scream tore through the silence, and he realized that Mei had heard him. Her salt circle had been sealed, but Ellie had retreated to join the pack so she stood alone, in the shadows, feet away from them. "Don't leave me! He's here. Reece can see him, can't you, Reece? Please." Mei's voice cracked as she dropped to her knees and curled herself into the smallest ball possible, pressing her face down into her lap. Her wails continued, muffled by her own body. "Don't leave me! He'll get me, he'll get me, he'll kill me…"

"Jesus." Hugo's voice was hollow. "I thought she was the sensible one."

"Same," Toni agreed, her voice wobbly. "What do we do?"

"Where's her bag?" Ellie snapped. The group looked

around the hall. Reece knew that like him, Hugo didn't have one. Callum had what looked like his old schoolbag dangling from one shoulder while Toni and Ellie had stayed glued to theirs. The candlelight did nothing to illuminate more than two feet in front of them – how the hell did olden days people live like this? Even so, it was clear there was no bag.

"Mei?" Reece crouched down in front of the tightly knotted girl. It seemed to him that the darkness was pressing down on her, making her even smaller. "Mei," he repeated, trying to keep his voice level, gentle, "do you remember what you did with your bag?" A mumble escaped the salt circle and Reece gritted his teeth in frustration. The others were pacing behind him, staying far away from the curtains, which still swayed gently. "Mei, I can't hear you. You need to look at me." She moved in slow motion, peeling her blotchy face away from her forearm. Her glasses hung at a wild angle and all Reece could see were her huge, black pupils. Her voice was just as hollow as her eyes.

"Library." The word scratched the air and Reece craned his neck around at the others.

"Hell no," Toni spat. "I'm not getting it."

"Nobody asked you to." Ellie shot her a sidelong glance as she stopped beside Hugo. "We'll go, won't we?" Reece clocked the light hand on posh boy's arm and the flush of his cheeks. Not even the lack of light could hide Hugo's crush.

"Erm, yeah, OK," he choked, still looking down at Ellie's hand.

"We can all go," Reece suggested. He wasn't going to let Hugo snag the hot girl so easily, no chance.

"No!" Mei wailed from the circle. She was sat up on her knees now, both hands pulling at the hem of her top again, her fingers twisting it in knots. "I can't leave the circle!" She broke into ugly sobs and, for the first time, Reece wondered how old she actually was. "Don't … leave … me…" She lost it again, huge moans wracking her body.

Reece hadn't even thought about it being real until that point. She could leave the salt, couldn't she? It was just a game after all. But she was so worked up, so scared…

"What do we do?" Callum asked quietly. The five of them moved closer, Mei's sobs echoing through the large hall. "She's lost all sense of reason. Does anyone have an extra candle?"

"Oh, God, of course! Wait," Ellie dropped her shoulder, allowing one of the handles of her tote to slide off. She transferred her candle carefully to the other hand and started to dig around as Toni begrudgingly swung her little backpack round and unzipped it. "I was sure I had a couple of spares." Ellie rummaged a little more. "I … I can't find them."

"Mine is gone too," Toni spluttered, showing the contents of her little patent bag. "I brought another and some more matches, but they're missing as well…" she trailed off, looking at the group around her. "Who the hell has been in my bag?" she demanded, face wrinkled in fury.

"It wasn't one of us," Mei's voice piped up, dull and monotone once more. "It's him. He's doing this so we can't play, so he can … can…"

"Oh, please," Reece said out loud, trying to inject his voice with confidence, even though his spine had turned to jelly. "He's not real. The Mid—"

"DON'T SAY IT!" Callum and Ellie burst out at the same time. Hugo had lost any pink glow from his cheeks and even Toni winced.

"Don't say his name," Ellie whispered. "Just in case."

"Fine." Reece felt stupid, like a kid who had just been told off for swearing or something. "Well, we have to do something." He checked the time, turning his wrist just enough so the candle illuminated the watch face. "There's two and a half hours of this left. We need to sort her out."

"What do you think we should do?" Hugo asked. Reece almost felt bad at how genuinely worried about Mei he seemed.

"I don't have my inhaler," Mei's small voice wheezed in the darkness. "I need my bag, but you can't all go. Someone stay with me, please?"

The five remaining players looked at one another.

"Fine." Reece took charge. "Ellie, you should stay with Mei." She went to argue, but he held up a hand. "Your blood sugar will be more stable if you stay still, right?"

"Well, yeah, I guess." She didn't look happy, but Reece took it as a win anyway.

"And she feels safe with you," he said. Ellie nodded so he resumed giving out orders. "The rest of us will go and find Mei's bag. Safety in numbers and all that." Hugo, Callum and Toni exchanged looks and finally each of them nodded in agreement.

"Fine," said Callum, tapping a hand on Reece's shoulder. "Good plan." Reece felt a little bit of pride blossom in his stomach.

"Be careful, you guys." Ellie took her place beside Mei and started pacing around the girl in the salt circle. She looked at the smaller girl pointedly. "Don't be long, yeah?"

"Quick as we can," Hugo said as they began to walk towards the doorway.

Reece hid a smirk as the other boy fired off some kind of salute. What a dweeb.

Callum led them out into the upper hallway and hesitated.

"What now?" Reece asked. "Don't tell me you want to stay too?"

"It's not that." Callum faltered, looking at the staircase and then back to the corridor they had come down earlier. "What if her bag isn't in the library? We peeked into all the rooms on the way up, it could be in one of those. It might even be in the hut we started in. I don't remember seeing it, do you?"

Reece shook his head.

"No," Toni said quietly.

"Me either." Hugo shrugged.

Callum looked at the stairs again. "In which case, these stairs are the fastest way back to the beginning. If we *all* do the walk we just did up here and back again, covering every single room, it's going to take for ever."

"Spit it out." Toni sighed.

"Spit what out?" Reece asked, watching Toni sidle up to Hugo. Seriously, what was the appeal of this guy? Was it because he was loaded?

"The line," Callum answered as Toni groaned. "You know, the line that someone says in a scary movie that makes you scream at the TV."

"Sorry, mate, you've lost me. I don't really watch scary movies," Reece admitted, embarrassed.

"Well, in that case, allow me." Toni lifted the candle so it illuminated her dark lips as she affected a high-pitched, breathy voice. "Oh no, what shall we do now?"

Reece could hear the smirk in Callum's voice as he responded. "I think we should split up."

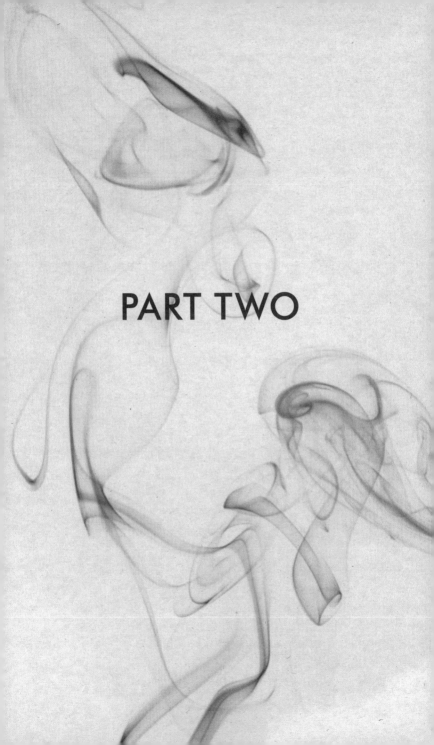

PART TWO

25/10/2021 23:45

WitchesBrew_2007: Hey, guys. Feeling pretty nostalgic tonight and thinking about all the creepy pasta stories I read as a kid. Ready to go down a rabbit hole — hit me with your faves! Games specifically. Trying to organize some Halloween fun...

MindMannequin_X07: Ooh, not been on here in for ever, but got to recommend the Eleven Mile Game. You want a link?

WitchesBrew_2007: Please!

MindMannequin_X07: No problem.

MindMannequin_X07: www.gamesyoushouldntplay.com/eleven-mile-game

MindMannequin_X07: Enjoy!

WitchesBrew2007: Thanks — I'll check it out now!

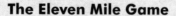
The Eleven Mile Game

Want to scare yourself silly? Or maybe go on a bit of a road trip? Well, in this ritual game you can do *both*. Yay! Just follow the rules and you'll get a reward at the end … if you reach your destination *alive*, that is.

Tell me more...

You'll need a few things before you start the game. Each item is <u>super</u> important and must be as close as physically possible to the description listed here for the ritual to work. If it's not, nothing will happen. Waste of time, right?

So what do I need?

Apart from nerves of steel, you will need the following items:

- A car. Make sure the petrol tank is FULL – you do not want to run out.
- A car radio, or some kind of radio frequency connected to the car.
- Your car must have a roof. If you have a soft top, make sure it's closed properly. No open sunroof either.
- At least one other person to go with you.

That's it! As long as your car is functioning, full of petrol and has no windows missing, you're ready.

Are there any rules?

A few. Some are basic road safety and others are a little more … well, scary as hell. And, as an added disclaimer, the forfeit for breaking any of these rules is said to be DEATH. Cool.

1. DO NOT open a window or exit the car until the game is over.
2. DO NOT run out of petrol.
3. DO NOT summon a demon into the car no matter what. Because just NO.
4. DO NOT take any haunted objects with you. That would be bad.
5. DO NOT place any of your limbs outside of the vehicle at any mile – EVEN IF YOU ARE TOLD TO.

Say I still want to – how do I play?

It's pretty easy to start. Jump in the car with a friend, check that all of the windows and doors are shut and then set off. You will want to drive out of the city, or to a quiet, rural area close by. When you get there, a road will eventually appear on the right-hand side of the street. You'll know it's your road if it doesn't appear on the map or it doesn't have a name. Make sure your radio is OFF and take the right turn.

God speed for the next eleven miles.

What happens now?

Technically, all you have to do is drive, stay calm and follow the rules. But these things are sent to try us, so you'll find yourself tested at each mile. This is what to look out for:

- Mile one: It's gonna get cold. Wrap up and put the heating on.
- Mile two: No, really, put the heater on or weird things will happen to your body.
- Mile three: Those shadows out there in the trees? They're not human, no matter how they look. IGNORE THEM.
- Mile four: The voices will begin. Don't listen to them – and certainly don't do anything they tell you.
- Mile five: A glowing moon will appear over a large, calm lake. It will look inviting. DO NOT stop.
- Mile six: Your radio will turn on. IGNORE IT.
- Mile seven: There will be whispers from the back seat. DO NOT LOOK BEHIND YOU.
- Mile eight: Your headlights will flicker or maybe even go out. Slow down and be safe but don't stop. You do not want them to catch up with you.
- Mile nine: The car is going to stall. DON'T PANIC, but you need to close your eyes until you can restart the car. Do not open them until the engine is working again and you can drive.
- Mile ten: DO NOT LOOK IN ANY OF THE MIRRORS.
- Mile eleven: You'll lose power a bit but keep driving

until you reach a red light. When it turns to green, you should feel the power come back and drive past some old-fashioned buildings. Keep going until there is a brick wall directly in your path. Stop the car.

What do I get out of all this?

Your reward, silly. Once you've stopped the car, say your wish out loud. You'll feel dizzy and may even black out, but when you come round, you'll be parked outside of the place you started. If you wished for an object, check the boot and the back seats – it might be there. If it's not an object, give it a few minutes and it should happen. Have fun!

ELLIE

"Split up? Are you joking?" Ellie could almost feel Hugo's panic as he backed into the hall. The poor guy looked terrible.

"What's going on?" Ellie asked.

Hugo turned to her with wide eyes and pointed at Callum, who now hovered in the doorway. "He," Hugo spat, his candle shaking dangerously, "wants us to *split up*. Have you ever heard anything so ridiculous?"

"I promise it'll be so much faster," Callum reassured him, stepping into the hall. His candle flickered, casting long, thin shadows on to the door frame above him. "Just go as quickly as you can without compromising the candle. We can all check different areas and get back here as soon as possible. Deal?"

Ellie avoided Hugo's gaze as he glanced around in panic. Callum was right.

Silence echoed through the room; even Mei was quiet.

"Fine," Hugo finally said, muttering something unintelligible under his breath.

"Great." Callum turned to Ellie and her charge. Mei had curled herself back into a tiny ball on the floor, and Ellie wasn't really sure what she should do about it. "We'll be back before you know it. Just, you know" – he motioned down to Mei, and Ellie was sure he did a cartoon gulp before finishing his sentence – "make sure she stays in the salt circle."

"No problem." Her voice echoed in the dark hall, despite the words feeling small in her throat. Tension knotted in the pit of her stomach as she watched the others leave again, the room growing smaller and smaller as each beacon of light departed. Finally, there were only the two of them left and all Ellie could see was what her small candle illuminated.

"They'll be back soon," she said out loud as she paced close to Mei, more to herself than anything. Just to hear the sound of a living voice rather than to make a statement. "And then we can start moving again."

"Can you sit with me?" The other girl's voice was barely audible.

Ellie sucked in a deep breath as she watched her candle burn. It was a steady, strong flame, not flickering or waning. She made a decision. "Sure." She walked to the edge of the salt circle and crouched carefully before sitting back and crossing her legs. She kept her bag firmly attached to her shoulder. "But if the flame starts to flicker, I have to move, OK?"

"OK." Mei slowly uncurled once more and sat up, mirroring Ellie's position. She pulled a sleeve down over her hand and removed her glasses, polishing them slowly with the fabric. Ellie watched in silence. It was clear Mei wanted to tell her something – she just had to wait for her to be ready. She watched quietly as Mei held the lenses out for inspection, checking for smudges before replacing the wide golden frames on the bridge of her nose. She tucked her other hand into a sleeve too and placed both covered hands in her lap. "Thanks for staying."

"Of course," Ellie said automatically, trying not to think about the dark expanse at her back. "We couldn't leave you alone, could we? And the others will be back soon." The words sounded hollow to her. She hoped they sounded at least a little bit reassuring to Mei. "How's your chest now?" she asked. "Better?"

"A little." Mei nodded.

"Hopefully they'll get your bag and you can take your inhaler. Come on, let's distract ourselves until they get back. Tell me about you – what do you like to do? Apart from" – she circled a finger in the air – "all *this*."

"I guess I don't really do much," Mei said. "I go to

normal school during the week and Chinese school on Sundays. Apart from that I study a lot – I want to be a solicitor. Well, my dad wants me to be a solicitor."

"That's cool, and you're definitely smart enough. What would you rather do, though?"

"What do you mean?"

"You said your dad wants you to do law. What would you choose to study instead?"

"Journalism, I guess. I love mysteries and researching. It's not as stable a career as my dad would like, though. So, law it is."

"Well, you never know. Maybe you could combine the two: work for a student paper at uni or something."

"Yeah." A bit of colour was returning to Mei's cheeks. "Maybe."

"So…" Ellie tried to change the subject, keep her talking. "What about the summer holidays? What do you do then?"

"I spend a lot of them in Asia with my mum's family. My grandparents and some of my cousins still live out there."

"Your mum's family? Is your dad not Chinese?"

"No, why did you think that?"

"Er…" Ellie felt her cheeks heat up as Mei realized the assumption she had made.

Mei let out a hollow laugh. "What, because he pushes me to study? Ha, no to *that* stereotype. Dad is whiter than you and probably has fewer qualifications. He's just pushing me to do all the things he could never achieve." Mei winced. "Wow, that was kind of harsh. I didn't mean it, I love him and he just wants the best for me, but I just wish he'd let up sometimes, you know?"

"So what does your mum think?"

"Mum's the total opposite. She's a ceramic artist and she gets kind of wrapped up in her work and the gallery shows. Dad does most of the day-to-day stuff apart from Chinese school. And I only really go there because mum teaches the language class. I guess I'm kind of boring."

"Boring?" Ellie smiled. "I wish I could speak another language and travel in the holidays. It sounds amazing! I'm lucky if we can afford a week in a caravan in Wales every year. Maybe it's time to talk to them, though, let them know you have interests you want to pursue."

"I guess. Thanks, Ellie." Mei's shoulders had relaxed a little, but her eyes still darted around the dark hall. Ellie fought the urge to look behind her and checked her flame instead. Still strong. "Ellie? Can I ask you something?"

"Sure." The cold of the floor was starting to seep in through her denim shorts and she shuffled slightly. "Go for it."

"Do you…" She paused, wide eyes staring over Ellie's shoulders. She dropped her voice. "Do you think all this is real?"

Ellie froze.

"I don't know." She tried her best to keep her voice level. "I've never played it before."

"I know." Mei sighed. "Me either. But if it is real … do you think…"

"What?"

"Do you think if I tell you my secret, then the … then *he* won't be able to use it against me?"

"Oh. I don't really know. Maybe?" She narrowed her eyes. "Why? Is it that bad?"

"No." Mei said quickly, shaking her head. "Not bad."

"Then do it. Tell me."

"It's kind of embarrassing."

"I won't laugh." Ellie raised her free hand and extended her little finger to Mei. Her pale green nail polish glowed almost white in the gloom. "Pinkie promise."

Mei stared at Ellie's finger for a beat too long. She was about to pull back when Mei pushed her hand out of its sleeve and wrapped her pinkie finger around Ellie's. The girl's skin was cold and clammy. Ellie shivered.

"Pinkie promise," Mei echoed, twisting their wrists slightly. The candlelight caught the etching on Ellie's wrist, poking out from beneath a thin, silver bracelet and the strap of her watch. "Hey, is that a tattoo? Cool. How did you manage to get that if you're not eighteen?"

Ellie dropped her finger. "How do you know I'm not eighteen?"

"Oh, sorry, I…" Mei tripped over the words. "I don't; it was just a guess. I kind of thought some of the others were older. Are you? Eighteen, I mean?"

"No," Ellie admitted begrudgingly. "I almost am."

"So, how'd you get the tattoo?"

"My natural charm," Ellie joked, thinking back to the day she'd walked into the tattoo studio with her best friend. If she was being honest, it was her friend that had the natural charm, not Ellie. People loved that girl. "Well, that and a decent fake ID."

"That is so cool," Mei breathed, temporarily distracted. "What does it mean?"

"That's kind of private," Ellie said, turning her wrist back towards her body so the little infinity symbol was out of Mei's sight.

"Oh, sorry. Will you tell me if I tell you my secret?"

Ellie tilted her head, considering. Finally, she nodded. "Maybe. But you go first."

"OK," Mei whispered. Ellie looked down at her candle flame, still large and strong. They were safe.

For now.

"I'm not quite eighteen, either."

Ellie pressed her lips together to hold back a smile. She already had Mei pegged as the baby of the group. Sixteen at the most.

"That's OK," she soothed as Mei's face crumpled. "I won't tell anyone, I promise."

"It's … it's not that." Mei's voice was starting to wobble again, and she took some deep, jerking breaths to steady herself. "I'm quite a bit younger than eighteen."

"Oh?" Ellie was only half listening now – had her candle flame just flickered?

"Yeah. I'm … still at high school." Ellie stayed quiet as a gust of cool air made the flame dance in front of them. "Ellie?"

"I have to get up. Now." She pushed herself up to standing as carefully as she could manage, Mei copying her movements from inside the circle. When they were both standing, Ellie looked down at Mei. The tiny girl was shaking from head to toe. "Mei, exactly how old are you?"

"Ellie, your candle…"

"How old are you?" Ellie demanded, her hand shaking. The flame was flickering wildly now, and she started digging in her bag for the matches. As if on cue, the air stilled for a second before being torn apart by a scream that echoed up from the bowels of the building.

"Oh God, someone's in trouble! Here," Ellie thrust the candle at Mei as she rooted for the matches.

The flame snuffed out, but not before Ellie saw the glint of tears pouring down Mei's cheeks.

"I'm fourteen," she whispered.

26/10/2021   00:05

WitchesBrew_2007: As cool (and terrifying) as the Eleven Mile Game seems, I don't think it has "party" written all over it, do you?

MindMannequin_X07: Fair point. Plus, you need a car.

WitchesBrew_2007: I actually have one! It's pretty beaten up, but I'm taking my test soon.

BANdit: You have a car? Cool.

WitchesBrew_2007: Yeah. It's older than me, but it runs. Freedom, right?

BANdit: Hell yeah.

WitchesBrew_2007: You know any creepy pasta games, @BANdit? Or anyone else on here tonight?

BANdit: Let me think.

Grimilim: Hey. What about that Three Kings game? You heard of that one? You do it at home, so you won't need a car.

146

WitchesBrew_2007: Are there mirrors involved? Sounds vaguely familiar…

Grimilim: Here: www.gamesyoushouldntplay.com/thethreekings game

WitchesBrew_2007: Perfect – will look now. Thanks!

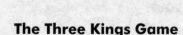

The Three Kings Game

Want to know what the future holds? Or maybe even find out what people really think of you?

Then this might be the ritual for you.

Tell me more...

This game is said to summon two other versions of you. Maybe it's part of a multiverse or a parallel universe, or they could even be your doppelgangers, who knows? You ask questions and they will answer — but beware! One is the queen, but the other is the fool. In essence, one of them always tells the truth, and one of them always lies. The problem is — you don't know which is which.

So what do I need?

Quite a bit, actually, so you might need to plan ahead for this one.

- A partner. They won't play; they're your safety net. Choose wisely!
- A large, quiet room. An attic or basement would work perfectly.
- Candles & a lighter.
- A bucket of water (we'll get to that).
- An electric fan.

- Three chairs.
- Two large mirrors (not too big, they need to rest on the chairs).
- An alarm clock (analogue if possible – we know these rituals work best without tech).
- A small item that means a lot to you.

Are there any rules?

A few. They will make more sense when you know how to play the game, but here are some things to bear in mind:

- DO NOT consume alcohol or drugs in the days preceding – these could have negative consequences.
- DO NOT PLAY if your alarm did not go off at exactly 3:30 a.m. Also, if the door is shut, the fan is off, or you don't make it by 3:33 a.m. IT WILL NOT BE SAFE TO CONTINUE. You, your partner and anyone else in the house will need to leave IMMEDIATELY and only return after sunrise.
- If you get an answer, DO NOT look directly in the mirrors. You should also remember that these answers may be false.
- DO NOT move until your partner calls you at 4:34 a.m.

Say I still want to – how do I play?

Well, first of all you have to set up the room. At 11:00 p.m., place the three chairs in a triangle, facing each other. Your chair (now your "throne") should be facing north, so you'll have to figure that out. Then prop the mirrors on the other two chairs and arrange them so that they reflect both you and each other. When you take your throne, you should be able to look directly ahead but see both of your reflections in your peripheral vision.

Place the water in front of you, but just out of reach. Then set up the fan behind your chair. You want it turned on low but kept stationary, not wafting around. You're not in a music video. Grab the other bits (candles, lighter, alarm clock and special item) and leave the door open. Then go to bed. Set your alarm clock for 3:30 a.m., snuggle your item and go to sleep. Your partner will want to sleep now, too. When your alarm goes off, grab your kit, light a candle and get your ass in that throne before 3:33 a.m. – but not until you make sure that it's safe to proceed. Now – your ride or die. They need the alarm clock. It's their job to sit outside the door and wait until 4:34 a.m. They will call your name to end the ritual. If you do not respond when they do this, they should enter the room and throw the bucket of water over you.

NOTE: <u>You should be able to trust this person with your life</u>. And not to fall asleep.

What happens now?

Now, my dear, you play.

Light your candle and use your body to protect the flame from the fan. You may now ask your questions, but be careful, as you might learn things you wished you didn't...

What do I get out of all this?

The wisdom of the universe ... the meaning of life ... or a mirror phobia for evermore.

Have fun!

MEI

"Hang on," Ellie said.

Mei forced her hand to stop shaking as Ellie struck a match. The candle was relit and taken from her hands in nanoseconds. Ellie seemed almost unshakable, and Mei was glad she had been the one chosen to stay with her.

"Who was that?" Mei sniffed, her nose cold and numb. "They sounded scared. I don't think I could ever scream that loud."

"I don't know, it sounded like Toni, maybe? Unless the guys can scream in falsetto." Ellie pushed the matches into the pocket of her shorts. The denim was so tight Mei could see the outline of the rectangular packet in the denim.

Mei tucked her hands back into the sleeves of her top,

not caring that she'd get told off for stretching out the cuffs. Ellie's candle had stopped flickering now, but the big assembly hall was getting colder by the minute. She stared at the other girl, willing Ellie to stay, wishing she hadn't just admitted to being wildly underage.

"I have to go and see if everyone is OK," Ellie started, locking eyes with Mei. She knew it. Any second she would be left there alone, in the dark. Her chest began to rise and fall a little faster than normal.

Did that curtain just move?

"Mei, are you listening to me?" Mei tore her eyes away from the drapery and tried desperately to focus on what Ellie was saying. "I won't go far, I promise, just until I see someone else and make sure they're checking it out. OK?"

"I..." Whatever Mei was going to say stuck in her throat. She didn't have the words for how terrified she was, but she felt it with every fibre of her being. "OK."

"Do you want the matches? For a little bit of light?"

"No." Mei's voice was hoarse, so she tried clearing her throat, to at least sound like she was in control of herself. "No, you'll need them, in case your candle goes out again."

"I could light a match for you before I go?"

Mei shook her head. "No point. It will almost be out before you get to the door. Don't waste it." She tried to push down her despair as Ellie headed towards the doors, willing away the panic that was beginning to curl around her like a snake. The shadows started to creep in immediately, long, suffocating fingers of darkness stretching towards her from every corner of the room. She swallowed hard.

"Mei?" Ellie paused at the doorway, her silhouette carved out by the candle. "Are you really only fourteen?"

Mei nodded, tears of embarrassment threatening to spill again. "I'm sorry."

"Oh, honey. It's OK. Wait right there and I promise once I get back I won't leave you again. We'll stick together like glue, OK?"

Mei sniffed. "Promise?"

"Promise."

"Ellie?"

"Yeah?" the older girl asked, one foot already in the hallway.

"Do … do you have a secret?"

Ellie paused before turning back to face Mei. It was hard to read her face from this distance.

"Yeah." The other girl's voice was stony as she headed through the doorway and disappeared from view. "Yeah, I do."

Mei clung to the sound of Ellie's footsteps. Soon – too soon – they faded away, until all she could hear was her own breathing. She mulled over Ellie's response. What had she meant? Why didn't she just tell Mei what her secret was? Mei couldn't read half the people here tonight, not that she was usually any good at stuff like that. Most of her friendships were online and she kept to herself at school. The only one she really trusted here was Callum and he was … well. She didn't know where he was.

And now someone was in danger.

Mei kept her eyes trained in the direction of the door, her ears straining for any sign of footsteps outside that might mean someone was coming back for her. She turned her body away from the curtains that lined the long wall and shifted her weight from one foot to the other.

The school was silent.

"Come on," she whispered, hoping the sound of her own voice would help, but it sounded so small, so lost in the dark, that she didn't try again.

Hours – confirmed to actually be minutes by her watch – crept past in silence. Mei's ears were starting to ring as she watched the little glow-in-the-dark hands move at a glacial pace. She focused all her attention on them, trying her best to ignore the tightness in her chest and block out the rest of the room. The watch was tight, even on her small wrist, a souvenir from a holiday in Hong Kong. Six, maybe seven years ago? She'd been about eight at the time. Mr Fluff had come from the same trip. They'd been to Ocean Park to see the new baby pandas at the zoo there and, of course, baby Mei refused to leave without her very own. Her grandparents had caved and bought it for her immediately. She smiled at the memory, remembering how huge the black and white bear had seemed when they left the gift shop. She thought of him now, alone and cold in her bed.

She wanted to go home.

"Mei?"

Her back stiffened at the sound of her name. "Ellie? Oh, thank God." She almost sobbed in relief. Now she could just light her spare candle and—

"Mei!" The voice came again, more urgently this time. Mei felt a cold prickle of fear on the back of her neck. The doorway was empty.

The voice was coming from inside the room.

"No," she whispered. It wasn't real. This *couldn't* be real. She screwed her eyes shut but her brain flooded with intrusive thoughts. Figures closing in on her, dropping from the ceiling like broken puppets, limbs bent at unnatural angles with smiles that were far too big for their faces. Every creepy pasta nightmare she'd ever seen on screen manifested itself into this room, crawling, dragging and creeping closer…

Mei forced her eyes open.

Nothing. No one was there. Nothing was there.

Then she felt it. A cool, targeted puff of air.

Someone was breathing on her neck.

"Meiiiiiiiiiii."

"Stop it!" she screamed, whipping around to an empty room. "Who's there?"

"Mei!" A hiss this time, but friendlier, more comfortable. "Mei, we have your bag."

"Who's there?" The voice was male, maybe? But it was so hoarse, so low, she couldn't quite figure out who it was. The voice was buried deep in the shadow at the other side of the room.

"Come on, quickly. Everyone's in the art room." The art room – that was just next door, they'd passed it on the way in. It wasn't far. Her toes twitched and she looked at her feet, at the white ribbon of salt that surrounded her.

She shouldn't move.

"Can't you bring it to me?" She was proud that her voice didn't betray her nerves.

Silence.

"Reece? Callum?" Nothing. "Hugo? Is that you?"

"Hurry up." At the opposite side of the room, Mei watched as a crack of light bloomed into being. There was another door there; they hadn't noticed it before. "Come on."

She hesitated. She wasn't meant to leave the circle. And the game said not to listen … but it *sounded* like one of the boys. And if it wasn't, surely she could be back here in a flash if the art room was only next door? She glanced around her. She was fed up with standing in the dark alone. She closed her eyes and clenched her hands tight, which meant she didn't see the door open further, or the shadows that played along its wooden panels.

Legs trembling, Mei took a deep breath.

And stepped out of the salt circle.

26/10/2021   00:24

WitchesBrew_2007: I really love that website; I need to read some more! Can't believe I haven't been on it before. And love the sound of that game! But looks like it's only for two people … be pretty hard to do at a party?

Grimilim: Yeah, I guess. You want more players, then?

WitchesBrew_2007: Yeah – I'm trying to organize an epic Halloween bash. There should be loads of people going so I kind of need something for everyone.

BANdit: Oooh, did someone say Halloween party? So cool! Where are you having it?

WitchesBrew_2007: This abandoned cinema near me. It's proper old-school: it has one of those little popcorn kiosks and red velvet seats in the screening rooms. My parents used to love it there – apparently that's where they went for their first date, which is equally lame and cute.

BANdit: Awww, that is kinda cute. So, you want a game like hide and seek then, I reckon. Sounds like there are loads of rooms there. Perfect for hiding.

Grimilim: An abandoned cinema party?! That really is epic. Are people doing costumes and stuff?

WitchesBrew_2007: Oh, yeah, the whole thing. I'm still trying to decide what to go as, though. Too many options!

Grimilim: Tell us when you decide!

WitchesBrew_2007: 😊

MindMannequin_X07: I'm sure there is a hide and seek game on that website – think it says that it's only for one person, but I don't see why more couldn't play? Go and have a look – it's called Hide and Seek Alone, something like that.

Grimilim: This is it: www.gamesyoushouldntplay.com/onemanhideandseek

One Man Hide & Seek

This one appears to originate in Japan and, let me tell you, as a massive Manga fan, I'm pretty tempted to play this one myself. I can totally see Junji Ito writing a graphic novel about it. I'm not entirely ready to sacrifice one of my stuffed animals, though.

Tell me more...

This game is pretty much what it says on the tin – hide and seek. Only you play with a toy that has a spirit trapped inside it. Kind of like playing party games with Annabelle. "Why would you want to do that?" you ask me. You've got me there. This one seems to be all about thrill-seeking. You should probably only play this if you've run out of cars to hijack or things to set on fire.

So what do I need?

Oh, the usual. You're gonna need:

- One stuffed doll or animal with limbs – that part is important.
- A bag of uncooked rice.
- Nail clippers.
- Needle and red thread.
- A knife/pair of scissors.
- A bath!!! (**Not** a shower.)
- A glass of saltwater.

- Sage stick.

Are there any rules?

OF COURSE there are. Here we go:

- Before it gets to 3 a.m. you need to make sure ALL the lights in your home are switched off.
- Name your toy. DO NOT give it your name – in fact, don't name it after anyone you know. That would be … well, not good. A made-up name will work just fine. May I suggest *Lil' Horror Goblin*? Cute.
- The start time is … you got it, 3 a.m. on the dot. You don't need any other players – hence the name – but there are no rules to say you *can't* have more than one.
- You should NOT: turn on the lights, lock any doors, make noise or leave the house.
- You should carry the saltwater if you need to leave your hiding place.
- Oh, one more thing. You MUST complete the game. It would be *bad* if you didn't finish. Not only that, it *cannot* go over two hours. Breaking either of these rules will place you in immediate jeopardy.

Say I still want to – how do I play?

I was afraid you'd ask that. This is the creepy bit. (OK – that's a lie – it's all creepy.) Take your equipment to the bathroom and use the knife/scissors to slice the stuffed toy open and take out the filling. When its poor, deflated shell is empty, replace the stuffing with the rice. Now, grab the nail clippers, cut off one of your fingernails and pop it in with the rice. Yes, I know, and yes, I'm sorry. Now, take the needle and thread and sew old stuffy up. When it's all sealed, wrap the rest of the thread around the toy and tie the ends in a knot. DO NOT cut the string. Now, fill the bath with water and when that's done, find a hiding place. You'll want to take your sage with you to cleanse the space. (Note: please source your sage responsibly or use another ethical alternative.) The saltwater and knife/scissors all go in this hiding place too. Back in the bathroom, repeat the phrase "*I (insert your name) am the first it*" three times. Fully submerge your new bestie in the tub and leave it there.

Now run.

What happens now?

You hotfoot it to your hiding place and count to ten with your eyes closed. Then grab your knife/scissors and go back to the bathroom. Take the doll out of the tub, say "*I have found you, Lil' Horror Goblin*", and cut the red thread that's binding it. Throw that sucker back in the bath and get the hell out of there. Seriously, go straight to your hiding spot and shut the hell up. I've warned you. The rice inside *Lil' Horror Goblin* is to attract spirits and the red thread is to bind them. When you cut that thread, you're letting loose whatever has taken hold

163

of the toy and **setting it free**.

Now, you go looking for them. Grab the cup, take a mouthful of the saltwater (DO NOT swallow) and leave your hiding place. Now look for the toy. You will probably want to try the bathroom first, but a word of warning:

LIL' HORROR GOBLIN MIGHT NOT BE WHERE YOU LEFT THEM. The stuffed toy is it now, which means IT is looking for YOU.

When you find the creepy little rice sack, pour the water from the cup on it and then spray the water in your mouth on top. Then say (or scream in maniacal relief) *"I WIN, I WIN, I WIN!"* Put the doll somewhere safe to dry out and then burn that MF. Discard the remains and wonder why you sacrificed your favourite Bernstein Bear for this effing game.

What do I get out of all this?

One less stuffed teddy in your collection and a fear of rice.

Have fun!

CALLUM

"You really didn't hear that?"

"Nah. I told you, I'm, like, fifty-eight per cent deaf in this ear." Reece flipped a finger backwards to indicate his right ear as he poked around the classroom they'd started in – they had come back to the hut.

Callum tipped his head and strained to hear the sound again, but the room was almost silent. The only noise was of Reece pushing chairs out of the way with a screech. Their efforts to find Mei's bag had failed.

"Nothing here, mate," Reece said. "Come on, let's go back."

"OK." Callum gave the room one last sweep with narrowed eyes before holding the door open for Reece.

He passed carefully, red tracksuit sleeves pushed up his forearms, one hand around his candle. Callum slowly followed him back through the makeshift corridor, down the hallway and into the foyer. His flame remained strong. Their footsteps echoed in the high space, and Callum tried to tune into any other noises. "I can't believe you didn't hear it. It sounded like a scream."

"Sorry." Reece started to climb the grand staircase in front of them.

"Whoa, where are you going?" Callum hissed, leaning over to tug the bunched-up arm of the other boy's top. This kid wasn't too clever, was he? "We need to check the other classrooms down here too. You know, in case that's where Mei left her bag."

"Sod that." Reece glared down at him and Callum realized he was still holding on to his sleeve. He pulled his hand away slowly. "I'm going back to the girls."

"No, come on," Callum pleaded. "We'll go this way, check quickly and be back before you know it, hopefully with Mei's bag. Then we can carry on playing." He checked his watch. "Look, it's almost quarter past one. If we go this way and be careful, we can be back with them by half past at the latest. Then there's just two hours left to kill." The last bit stuck in his throat. Bad choice of words. He took a deep breath and blew it out, regretting it immediately as his candle flame flickered slightly in the sudden breeze.

"Not a chance." Reece's eyes were on Callum's candle too. "It felt safer upstairs. Look at your candle."

"That was me! I just breathed out—"

"And you're hearing screams and whatever? Hello hallucinations. I don't think I want to stick with you any more. You might as well have a target on your back." Callum's mouth hung open. What was he supposed to say to that? "Look, mate" – Reece lowered his voice and leaned over the handrail – "the others have probably found the bag. We'll be safer in a group, right? Let's just go up and see who's back there."

Callum was torn. They could assume there was safety in numbers, go up and pace around the hall for two hours, watching Mei slowly lose it in that salt circle. Or they could do one more sweep of the corridor, which could mean finding her bag, which could mean them all being on the move again. He set his jaw and looked up at the other boy.

Reece was already halfway up the stairs.

"I'm going to check the corridor," Callum called up.

Reece didn't break his stride. "Whatever. You do you. I'll see you in a bit."

"Yeah." Callum stood in the growing darkness as Reece and his candle retreated further up the stairs, finally leaving his sight. His feet were itching to follow, especially now that he was alone.

He was so sure he'd heard a scream.

"I'll just go this way," he muttered to himself, ignoring the staircase and heading to the open door beyond it. The corridor they had walked down earlier stretched out in front of him, a dark expanse punctuated with yawning black mouths on either side. Callum closed his eyes, trying to centre himself. When he finally forced his eyelids apart, the mouths were nothing more than doorways, but the hallway still looked twice as long as he remembered it.

He took a tentative step forward, making sure his candle looked healthy. Years of memories began fighting for attention in his head. His mum had worked here since his dad left them when Callum was still a little kid. Since he had gone to the school around the corner, he would come straight here and do his homework while she cleaned. She loved working there and the staff loved her too. She'd knit them stuff or leave little chocolates on their desks at Easter and Christmas, or sometimes just after a busy week, so no one ever minded that her kid sat in one of the classrooms while she tidied up around them. One of the younger teachers even used to sneak him the good biscuits from the staffroom, which he loved. He smiled. His mum was one of life's good ones. She'd string him up if she found out he'd nicked her keys.

Callum braved a quick look into the part of the building where the music rooms were. The doors were all closed, their little windows reminiscent of the cells they had once been. They were so sinister. An eerie atmosphere surrounded them, like the past misdemeanours were left behind, even though the prisoners were long gone. He'd always hated these rooms, especially in the dark.

There was no sign of a bag in there anyway. He shuffled past, telling himself that he wasn't worried he would see a dark shadow slam itself into the windows or anything.

He moved quickly.

Both classrooms were as they had found them earlier – clean and tidy, chairs neatly stacked on top of tables. The way his mum had left it yesterday, no doubt. There were no obviously dropped bags anywhere that he could see.

That just left one place to check down here.

The library.

Callum's feet stopped at the threshold and his flame gave a little flicker. The room appeared empty, though it was a little brighter than the others thanks to those streetlights. A shudder ran down his back as he remembered the dark figure at the door, and he forced himself inside. Again, it was clean and tidy and the only thing out of place was the book Mei had picked up earlier. Callum collected it and slid it back on to the shelf it had come from, took one last glance around and headed to the doorway.

His candle started to flicker again.

"Oh, no you don't." He cupped his free hand around the flame. He stepped back into the hallway and pushed open the door to the stairwell when a breeze teased past him, raising the tightly curled hair at the nape of his neck until it almost hurt. He needed to get back upstairs.

The door closed behind Callum, trapping him in the stairwell as another gust of wind hit him. "Dammit!" He mounted the bottom step, the hand that should have been on the banister wrapped around the flame instead. Ancient security lights dotted the staircase, casting shadows on the steps but providing little light. He had to keep this candle lit. He *had* to.

"Callllllllluuuuuuuuummmmmmmmmm." The sound was all around him, so dense that he wasn't sure whether it was travelling through the air or if it was just in his head. The candle flickered again, and he let out an involuntary sob. He reached one leg up, trying to take the steps two at a time, but his shaking limbs misjudged the distance and before he knew it, his body started to tilt backwards.

"No!" He reached out to grab the railing, his shoulder wrenching uncomfortably in its socket as it saved him from the fall. He wobbled a little, but he managed to hold on and plant both of his feet back on the steps. He lifted the candle up in front of him, glad he hadn't dropped it, but it didn't matter.

A bare, blackened wick stared back at him.

"Oh, hell no." He panicked, fumbling for the matches. He tried his best to keep count in his head, but between scrambling in the tiny drawer and keeping the numbers straight, he had no idea how much time was going by. He was still trying to count when a bright white explosion rocked his sight, pushing him forwards on to his hands and knees, followed by a blinding pain in the back of his head. Callum blinked, once, twice. His body was working in slow motion, not keeping up with his racing thoughts.

Then the shadows swallowed him.

26/10/2021   00:45

WitchesBrew_2007: Oh, hell no. LIL' HORROR GOBLIN. I can't believe you let me look that up before bed, *@MindMannequin_X07*!!! I feel like I need to bleach my eyes. Just the thought of some little Chucky monster running around and slicing everyone's Achilles tendons makes me break out in a cold sweat!

WitchesBrew_2007: Oh god – and if there's more than one player, do you need more than one toy?

WitchesBrew_2007: JUST EVIL DEMON FLUFFIES RUNNING WILD IN AN ABANDONED CINEMA. NOOOOOOOOOOPE.

BANdit: I just read it too. Hard pass.

BANdit: Though I'm gonna copyright Lil' Horror Goblin for my rapper name.

WitchesBrew_2007: Lol.

BANdit: I really hope you don't have any of those creepy porcelain dolls in your room?

WitchesBrew_2007: Oh god…

BANdit: … wait…

BANdit: OMD YOU DO!

WitchesBrew_2007: Looks like I'm sleeping on the sofa tonight.

26/10/2021   08:57

@BANdit added the user @Miss_contrary06 to the thread.

BANdit: Hey, morning, @WitchesBrew_2007. Just added my friend @Miss_contrary06 to the chat, she knows tons of these games.

WitchesBrew_2007: Oh, cool, thank you. Hi @Miss_contrary06 *waves*. You got any suggestions for a game that a biggish group could play in a big space?

WitchesBrew_2007: I like your username btw!

Miss_contrary06: Hi! Aw, thanks. Yeah, I have a couple of ideas. This one can def be played with loads of people.

WitchesBrew_2007: This one doesn't have killer teddies called *Lil' Horror Goblin* in, does it?

Miss_contrary06: Ha, no (that is one creepy game, right?). Think you just need a camera for this one. It's called The Picture Game.

The Picture Game

Looking for a spooky party game that will suit any number of revellers? Then this is the one for you. You'll need an old school camera and – I'm not even joking – some alcohol. Talk about a party game!

Tell me more...

This ritual supposedly lets you invite spirits in and capture them on camera. There are a lot of warnings with this one, plus you need to be comfortable destroying the camera if needed, so best to use an old or at least cheap one, no family heirlooms or vintage pieces, please!

So what do I need?

A few items but they should all be fairly easy to source. The camera **with a flash** is the main piece of equipment and you only need one of these no matter how many people are playing. You also need:

- String or rope. The longer the better as you'll use it to make a circle to sit around.
- Scissors.
- One small mirror *per person*. You can't share mirrors; you must have one each.
- A drinking glass.
- Alcohol. Any kind will work, but wine is preferable.

175

Are there any rules?

They're probably classed as warnings rather than rules as mentioned above. They centre around the behaviour of the person taking the photograph, so you must pay close attention to how everyone is acting. I would suggest that you only play this game with those you know and trust – that way it is obvious if their attitude changes…

You should look for:

- Signs of distress. If a player starts to cry or feels sick, DO NOT allow them to take a picture; instead, they must skip that go. If they do manage to take a photo, you must NOT look at that picture, you must STOP the ritual and you must DESTROY the camera.
- Similarly, if a player starts to act in a way that is wildly out of character for them, or one or more players say they are scared, YOU MUST STOP PLAYING.
- Do not forget to end the ritual properly if you do stop. There are details further on about how to do this.

Say I still want to – how do I play?

This game must begin at midnight, the witching hour. You take the rope and knot the ends together, so when you lay it out on the floor it forms a circle. Now, put the glass in the centre of the circle and pour in the alcohol – fill it up, don't be shy. When this is done, everyone should take their seats on the outside of the circle. That bit is important! DO NOT step inside the rope once everyone is seated. Once each player is settled, they should place their mirror on the floor in front of them, so the reflective surface is pointing to the ceiling.

Finally, someone needs to turn out the lights.

What happens now?

Once you're all seated, everyone must close their eyes and **only then** hold hands with the people next to you (hoping it's the same person you saw a second ago...).

One at a time, the players must say "*I trust you*" out loud. It might help to choose someone to speak first and also decide which way around the circle to go. When you're all done, speak the following words in unison: "*The door is open, please come in.*" Then you can open your eyes and take turns with the camera. Each person must point the camera towards the glass in the centre and say "*I caught you*" while taking a photograph. Continue until every member of the group has taken three pictures.

When everyone has done that and you are ready to finish, it's time to close out the ritual. I know you might want to look through the pictures, but DON'T DO IT YET!

To close out, everyone must shut their eyes again and repeat "*It's time to go home*" as one. Then open your eyes and turn your mirror face down while someone turns on the lights (relieved sighs and smiles optional but encouraged at this point). Now someone needs to cut the rope, grab the drinking glass and empty it outside — a bare patch of dirt is ideal for this. Don't drink it...

What do I get out of all this?

Some snaps for the family album. Once you have cleaned up, you may look at the photographs. Really study them, look in the corners, at the dark space around the wine glass. See anything? No?

Try again.

Ah, there...

Have fun!

TONI

Wow. This posh git could *not* take a joke.

"You know it was funny," Toni sniggered. She'd even surprised herself; she didn't know she had a scream like that in her. She snapped the gum in her mouth. She needed a new piece – the taste had all gone from this one so it felt like she was chewing on a piece of rubber.

"Hilarious," Hugo replied dryly.

Toni lounged back on to the worktop in the make-shift kitchen area. They'd come down a different set of stairs to before and found nothing but the loos and staffroom. After poking around for a bit, Toni had got bored and tried to create a bit of fun on her own, but posho was having none of it. "What are you even doing, anyway?" she asked.

Hugo currently had his head – and his candle – in a long, tall cupboard, and was sniffing around like a truffle pig. She really hoped he didn't set his own hair on fire.

"Teachers always have biscuits," he said, closing the door and triumphantly brandishing a half-eaten packet of chocolate digestives. "Want one?"

"Ew, no." Toni wrinkled her nose at him, but her stomach betrayed her with a rumble that seemed to echo around the room. "Oh, fine." She held out a hand. "I'm bloody starving."

"Here." Hugo pushed a biscuit out with his thumb and Toni plucked it from the packet. "I'm sitting down."

"Shouldn't we keep moving?" Toni kept one wary eye on her candle as she nibbled the biscuit. It was a bit stale, but the chocolate melted on contact with her tongue, and she savoured the sweetness as she polished it off. She had skipped dinner. "We've been hanging around down here for ages."

"Nothing's happened yet, though, has it?" Hugo lowered himself on to a scratchy-looking sofa that was possibly brown but maybe dark blue. It was hard to tell in this light. Toni pushed herself off the counter and sat next to him instead, reaching for the packet he had left on the table and snapping a biscuit in half. "Why do people do that?" he asked.

"Do what?"

"Break a biscuit in half and leave it in the packet."

Hugo picked up another full one and took a bite that was almost the whole biscuit. "I bet most people go back and eat it anyway."

"I dunno." Why *did* she do it? Politeness? To look daintier, more girly in front of Hugo? She didn't usually care about that kind of stuff. "I guess I just didn't want to commit to the whole thing." Hugo turned his body towards her slightly, the edges of his mouth turned down in a frown.

"Commit? It's a biscuit, not marriage."

"What can I say?" Toni sighed, picking up the second half and trailing her tongue deliberately across the chocolate. "I like to keep my options open."

Hugo jumped from the seat as though an electric shock had passed through it, the flame on his candle blinking dangerously. "Er, we should probably go." He brushed his free hand on his jeans to dislodge the biscuit crumbs as Toni chuckled.

"What's the rush now?" She stood up too, making sure her body was only millimetres away from his. She could feel the heat radiating from him and almost purred. "We have all night." She leaned close and breathed into his ear. "And I taste like chocolate."

"Let's go, shall we?" The words burst out of him as he all but ran to the door. Toni didn't know whether to laugh or cry. He was proving a hard nut to crack; she had to think of a way to get him onside. If it all went belly-up, she

181

needed him to care about protecting her, not the others. Maybe it was her clothes; maybe he didn't like the all-black attire she was rocking tonight. She didn't usually look like this – she was just trying it on for size. "We should go and check on Ellie. And Mei," he rushed to add. Ahh, Ellie. Toni thought of the perky blonde and nodded. He definitely wasn't a fan of the goth girl look.

"She's cute," Toni said casually as she joined Hugo in the hallway. He was looking carefully each way, as if he was about to cross the road, his candle cradled to his chest like an injured bird.

"Mei? Yeah, she's a sweetie." He was clearly dodging the subject. "She seems a bit younger than us, don't you think?" He pointed to the right. "I think the main staircase is through those doors. Let's go and check the rooms we were supposed to and get back to the hall."

"Fine." Toni followed him carefully, wishing she'd brought the rest of the biscuits. "And not Mei – though, yeah, I think she's younger than she's letting on. I meant that Ellie's cute." Toni fell into deliberate silence, waiting for a response.

"Oh. I, uh, didn't really notice," Hugo stuttered. God, this kid was frigid. Toni wrapped her free hand in the back of his shirt, pulling him to a halt as she pressed against his back.

"Liar," she whispered, her voice like melted honey as she rested her head on his broad shoulder. "You want to screw her." Hugo visibly swallowed as Toni carried on, the fingers of her free hand inching the hem of his shirt up until her fingertips grazed the dip of his hipbone. "Hell," Toni continued as Hugo's breath quickened, "even *I* want to screw her." She slid one finger into his waistband. "Maybe we could share?"

Even in the darkness, Toni could see the effect she was having on him. He gave in and leaned back into her slightly before pushing away.

"Come on, we've been gone for long enough." He pulled the door open, not bothering to hold it for her. She caught it with her foot and glared at him as he began to walk up the main staircase. A tremor of irritation ran through Toni. He had pointedly rejected her.

Oh, he'd pay for that.

deddit

26/10/2021 09:11

WitchesBrew_2007: OMG I love that one! Mirrors in the dark are so freaky, though, I can't have any in my bedroom.

BANdit: Ikr? Cos, like, what if you moved **but your reflection didn't???**

WitchesBrew_2007: PRECISELY.

Miss_contrary06: Haha, pair of scaredy cats. Glad you liked it, though! You think it'll work for you?

WitchesBrew_2007: Yeah, maybe. I'm not 100% sold on it, though. What if you had to end it after like ten minutes?

Grimilim: That's a good point. I was pretty disappointed it didn't tell you to actually drink the wine…

BANdit: Ugh, wine is gross anyway.

MindMannequin_X07: Why don't we all have a look through the site real quick and see if there are any games that take a little while longer to play? I agree The Picture Game sounds awesome, but all it takes is one person to say, "I'm scared" and it's all over.

WitchesBrew_2007: GREAT idea, @MindMannequin_X07, that's if everyone is OK with that?

BANdit: Yep, always down for some spooky reading.

Grimilim: Me too. I love that site.

Miss_contrary06: Already on it!

WitchesBrew_2007: Amazing, thank you guys! I'd invite you all if I thought any of you were close to where I live – I bet you're all miles away, though. Right, I'm just off to an English lesson, catch up at lunch!

 **chat**

Inbox (@WitchesBrew_2007)
>Direct message request< 26/10/2021 09:33
From: Miss_contrary06
Hiya! Just thought I'd let you know you have a location tag on your posts – I wasn't sure if you meant to or not? Anyway, I live pretty close by! Dunno about the others, but this sounds like SUCH an epic party, would love to be involved :)

Outbox (@WitchesBrew_2007)
>Direct message< 26/10/2021 10:43
To: Miss_contrary06
OMG I had no idea! Not too great at this internet safety thing, am I? My primary school teachers would be so disappointed, lol. Cool, I'll send you an invite once we're all set! My bestie is making them; she's good with all that graphic stuff, I'm just the activities organizer. Thanks for helping with the games! XO

Inbox (@WitchesBrew_2007)
>Direct message< 26/10/2021 11:04
From: Miss_contrary06
No problem – I keep my location settings off to avoid the weirdos, lol. Looking forward to the invite – and your activities will be AMAZE. Better find me a costume!
Oh – almost forgot – go check out www.gamesyoushouldntplay. com/deadmanstag…

Deadman's Tag

Remember the thrill of playing tag as a kid? Running like the devil was behind you, so hard you felt like your heart would explode and your legs would fall right off? Yeah, me too. Brilliant, wasn't it?

Tell me more...

OK, imagine that adrenaline rush with one extra component.
    The person chasing you might not be a *person*...

So what do I need?

First, you need an open space. A field or meadow is ideal, as long as there are plenty of hiding places, but if you really want to up the ante you could choose to play in a graveyard. Just a thought. There's no limit on players, but everyone needs a torch, and a watch would be useful too.

Are there any rules?

Yes, and they're pretty specific, so listen up.

- DO NOT hide with anyone else.
- Use your torch as little as possible.
- Try to hide in SILENCE.
- You can move around as little or as much as you like. HOWEVER, if you sense someone else close by, you only have two options:

1. Stay where you are.
2. RUN. Whatever you sense may NOT be one of the other players.

- If you make it back to Home, you must touch it and shout "SAFE!" Now stay put and wait for all the other players to arrive back

Say I still want to – how do I play?

You need to start once the sun has set on a night where there is little to no moonlight. In my humble opinion, it's definitely worth planning ahead and checking when the next new moon is if you have a large group, that way you won't have to cancel or rearrange on the day.

Now, gather everyone at your chosen venue and decide where "Home" is. It should be something you can touch – a fence post, a tree, that kind of thing – and this is where you will all come back to after hiding. You must touch Home to be safe. Wait for it to fall dark and once the sun has fully set, all players must face out from Home while touching *at least* a fingertip to it, while one person says the following:

"We invite you to play with us. This is Home.
When the game starts, we have sixty seconds to hide,
then you can come and find us. When we all make
it Home, the game is over."

Everyone must shout *"You're it"*.

Then run.

Once you scatter, you should hide for the full sixty seconds before trying to make it back Home. DO WHATEVER YOU NEED to get there. Then you'll be safe.

What happens now?

To put it simply, you DO NOT want to be caught. You will be able to tell if another player has been caught and you should avoid them AT ALL COSTS. You can try to haggle for their souls, but you'll need something good to give in return. Keep your guard up and don't assume there's only one *it* playing with you when you head for Home. When you get there, check that all the people that are at Home are THE SAME PLAYERS WHO STARTED THE GAME. If they are not, then you should not proceed, but hide and try again. If everyone is back in their starting positions, one person must say *"We win! The game's over, thanks for playing with us."* Now, go home.

What do I get out of all this?

Epic bragging rights? I'm afraid this looks like another thrill-seeker special, but I think the real draw is the essence of the game. A gang of you can play like kids but with very adult consequences.

Though be warned, by playing this game, you have opened yourself up to an adversary who might want to play again.

Whether you like it or not. Have fun!

HUGO

Hugo tried to think of anything else as he desperately put some space between himself and Toni. Football, the first time he got kicked out of school, his grandfather's funeral. Anything to stop what felt like all of the blood in his body rushing to all the places it shouldn't be.

"I'm checking the library." Toni's voice was petulant, and Hugo took a deep, grounding breath through his nose before twisting his head to face her. "That's what we were supposed to do, right? I suppose you'd prefer it if I was a good girl who did as I was told." Toni pouted at him before disappearing into the dark hallway. Hugo hadn't even had time to answer.

Great.

He stood on the steps for a few seconds, his weight all on one foot as the other rested on the step above. He should keep climbing, go and check on Ellie – he pushed aside Toni's earlier words – and Mei, of course.

He didn't move.

"Great," he repeated out loud. He didn't really have a choice, did he? At least the girls upstairs were together, but Toni was on her own now. Stubborn mare. If something happened to her, if she got into an accident, or fell or something, then none of them would know. Not until they found her, anyway, and that could be hours from now. He clenched his jaw and stared into the depths of his flame. He would make sure he did the right thing this time.

She just needed to quit the OTT flirting. It made him nervous.

Hugo turned and faced down the stairs, shuffling heavy feet to the bottom, the dull thuds swallowed up by the shadows. He gave the staircase one last wistful glance before stepping into the hallway where Toni had disappeared. It was darker than he remembered. Much darker. He could barely see the end of it thanks to the thickening shadows. He checked his candle once more and took a deep breath, pushing his shoulders back like the therapist had shown him before he began to walk forwards. Very slowly. Very carefully.

He wished he could remember all the rules. Where had he put the list Mei had given him?

"Fancy seeing you here." The voice came from behind Hugo, to his left, and he automatically swung an arm around, his fist clenched as his body followed the punch. "Jesus!" Toni took a step back in the nick of time, Hugo's knuckles grazing the air where her face had been. "Calm your tits. I was just playing."

"Playing?" Hugo spat, adrenaline coursing through his veins so fast his thoughts could barely keep up. "You … you're not funny. You keep acting like this is all one big joke."

"Isn't it?" Toni shrugged as he looked at her in disbelief. "OK, whatever." She nodded at his candle. "Looks like you need to sort that."

"What?" Hugo looked at the tapered wax baton in his left hand, a small wisp of smoke dancing up from the still-glowing tip. His heart skipped a beat. "No."

"Tick tock!" Toni chirped brightly.

Hugo looked at her in dismay, tugging at the collar of his shirt. He couldn't remember how long he had. He wiped a hand across his forehead, pushing the hair back off his face. It had been boiling in here a second ago, but there was a definite sudden chill in the air. Shadows slunk on the edge of his peripheral vision, moving and twisting just out of sight. He flicked his eyes around the hallway but couldn't quite catch them in the act. They just crept in when he wasn't looking.

"Hugo? Hugo!" A pair of snapping fingers under his

nose pulled him around a little. "Don't have a bloody panic attack. Here." The crackle of a match pulled him fully back to the present, and he realized his breathing was fast and shallow, verging on being out of control. He tried to focus on regulating his breaths while Toni relit his candle, watching the orange flare with relief. She held up the match.

"Stick out your tongue."

"What?"

"You heard," she said.

Hugo was still partly on autopilot, so he obeyed, immediately regretting it as Toni pushed the flaming match on to the soft, pink flesh of his tongue. He pushed her hand away with a gasp.

"Hey!" He rolled his tongue around, his mouth filling with saliva to sooth the searing heat. "What the hell?" He took a step back and glared at her. "You're sick."

"And you're not on the verge of a meltdown any more." She actually had the audacity to look smug. She dropped the match on to the floor and sauntered ahead of him, one foot directly in front of the other, twisting her hips with each step so he could see every curve of her body.

Hugo stuck his tongue out and poked it with his finger, realizing it wasn't that sore any more. He sighed. She was completely out of control, but she was right, it had brought him back from the brink of an anxiety attack that would have helped precisely no one. Should she have done it? No. Was he glad she had? Yeah – kind of.

He wished she would stop walking like that, though.

"Library," Toni announced when she reached the end of the corridor. She leaned against the door frame, one hand behind her so that her chest was pushed out, the other holding her small candle up to illuminate it. Hugo hadn't noticed how low-cut her top was before. "This is where Mei said she'd left her bag, right?"

"Yeah, well she seemed to think so, anyway." Hugo said. He hesitated, waiting for Toni to go into the room, but it was clear she wanted him to squeeze past her. "Er, excuse me," he tried. She just grinned widely and held her candle out of the way.

"After you," she said. Her smile sliced through the dark. He eased past as chastely as he could manage, though he couldn't avoid brushing her chest with his arm. He cast his eyes around the room desperately, hoping he'd see the bag and they could get out of there before he did something he might regret. Toni pointed into the room. "There it is."

Hugo followed her finger and saw the little satchel half-hidden under the computer desk they'd been near when they drank his whisky. How he wished he had some left right now. He went to retrieve the bag and saw that the flap that should have covered the top had fallen open, so he peered inside, his free hand moving around the contents.

"What are you doing?" Toni appeared behind him, so

close he could smell the sweet, malty chocolate biscuit on her breath.

"Making sure there are actually candles in here." Hugo lowered his own light. It barely illuminated the edges of the jumble of contents, but he could see enough. "Yep, and not just one. She has six in here."

"A spare for each of us," Toni mused.

"Yeah." Poor Mei. He picked the satchel up. "Come on, let's get this back to her. Even if none of this is for real, it'll help her out, right?"

"That's really kind." Toni placed a hand on his arm and looked up from beneath her lashes, suddenly shy. "*You're* really kind." She looked different now, her face softer than it had been all night.

"I'm just doing the right thing," he said gruffly. "I'd do it for any of you."

Toni straightened up and tugged on his arm before he could pick the bag up, pulling him round to face her. He swallowed as she pushed him back a little, just far enough so that he bumped the computer table with the back of his legs, forcing him to sit down.

"We should go," he said weakly, but he didn't move. Toni stepped even closer, nudging one of his knees open with her leg and moving to stand in between them.

"In a minute," she murmured. She wasn't particularly short, but Hugo was pretty tall, so they were almost at eye level in this position. She carefully set her candle just out of reach, leaning over him as she did, then took his and did the same with it. He closed his eyes as she snaked her arms around his neck, goosebumps exploding down his back. "Just one minute," she promised. The little bag slid from his fingers, forgotten, as she pressed her lips to his.

Hugo gave into it then, her hot kisses trailing down his neck and towards his collarbone. He wrapped his arms around her waist and lifted her slightly, spinning her around until she was the one sitting on the desk. He leaned his weight on her, easing her backwards, so she was almost lying on the table, her legs wrapped around him, when there was the sound of a forced cough from the doorway.

They froze.

"Don't let me interrupt," Ellie snarled. "I'll just take Mei's bag and leave you to it."

26/10/2021   19:58

BANdit: Hey, guys. Is @WitchesBrew_2007 around tonight? I think I've found the perfect game for her get-together.

Miss_contrary06: Oh great – I sent her one before, but I've just realized you're meant to play outside … so not ideal for her party.

Grimilim: Was it Dead Man's Tag?

Miss_contrary06: Ha, yeah, how'd you know?

Grimilim: Read it today. Looks sick, but yeah, reckon it has to be outdoors. Everything else seems to be indoor, though.

20:08

WitchesBrew_2007: Hey guys! Sorry, I've just got back from a driving lesson. Getting close to booking my test now! I keep sitting in my car and just imagining the freedom…

BANdit: Awesome! That's so exciting.

WitchesBrew_2007: Thanks, it really is! So, you think you've found me a game? I'm all ears.

WitchesBrew_2007: Btw @*Miss_contrary06*, if we hadn't already started smuggling party stuff into the cinema, I'd be playing Dead Man's Tag in a graveyard FOR SURE. It's already on the list for next year!

Miss_contrary06: Happy to help :)

BANdit: Yeah, it's this one: www.gamesyoushouldntplay. com/them...

20:22

WitchesBrew_2007: Oh my life.

WitchesBrew_2007: This is the one.

WitchesBrew_2007: It's PERFECT.

The Midnight Game

This is a game that hits a little bit different. Again, it seems to be one for the adrenaline junkies out there, but rumour has it this ritual is ancient. As in, pre-Christianity ancient.

Tell me more...

The Midnight Game is classed as a Pagan ritual. (Remember, I'm only talking about Western traditions here. As much as I wish I was an expert in other cultures too, I can only comment on my own knowledge.) Old-timey people didn't really play this as a game. Oh no. This was serious business: a punishment for wrongdoers in the village. It was sort of a trial, if you will. If the "player" survived, they were innocent. If they didn't … well, they got their comeuppance.

So what do I need?

If you want to play you'll need a few things:

- One red candle.
- One other candle per player, plus at least one spare each. There is NO limit on players.
- Matches – NOT a lighter.
- Paper and a pencil/pen.
- A needle or other sharp object.
- Thumbtacks or drawing pins.

- Salt (as much as you can carry).
- Water and snacks (optional, but you'll be there for a while).
- A wooden door.

Are there any rules?

Naturally. The rules are there to keep you safe, so make sure you follow them religiously.

1. DO NOT turn on the lights.
2. DO NOT leave the building.
3. DO NOT go to sleep.
4. DO NOT carry a weapon.
5. If your candle goes out, relight it in ten seconds.
6. If you cannot, surround yourself with a salt circle immediately.
7. DO NOT leave the salt circle without a lit candle.
8. MOVE. Staying in one place is dangerous.

There is a bit more, but it's more advice than rules in my opinion. Ignore any noises you hear. Do not follow whispers. Try to stick together, because you are more vulnerable on your own. Watch your flame – if it flickers, or you feel a cold breeze, it means the Midnight Man is near. Move. If you can't because you have to stay in a salt circle, he will try to trick you into coming out of it.

Say I still want to – how do I play?

First of all, you need to find a place to play. This ritual used to be conducted in the home of the wrongdoer, but most houses are pretty small now, so any building with at least one wooden door will work. (Unless you live in a mansion, in which case just have a pool party, why don't you?)

When you have decided on a location, you need to gather your kit and your troops and sit in front of the wooden door. You don't necessarily have to walk through the doorway, but I like the symbolism, so I'd use an internal door if you can. Take your paper, pen, needle and a drawing pin. Now, write your name and prick your finger, then smear a bloody fingerprint next to your signature.

The Midnight Man will need to know whose blood he's tasting.

Now, stick it to the door with a pin, or Sellotape at a pinch. On a separate piece of paper, you have to write down the reason you're playing. It doesn't have to be a wrongdoing, but it does have to be something you'd rather other people didn't know. (Don't worry, if all goes well, you'll burn it and your secret will remain hidden.) Fold it up and put it somewhere safe, preferably about your person, in a zipped pocket or something.

What happens now?

Once each player has stuck their name to the door and hidden their "secret" paper, someone lights the red candle.

Then they knock on the door twenty-two times – the final knock MUST happen on the stroke of midnight. If it doesn't, DO NOT play, burn the papers and leave IMMEDIATELY.

If all goes well, blow out the red candle after the last knock and relight it immediately. Light your candle from this one and commence playing. If you can safely light all candles, all you have to do is move around the building and avoid the murderous entity for three and a half hours. Easy, right? Once 3:33 a.m. has passed, you close out the ritual by burning both pieces of paper and shutting the wooden door. Then you're done.

What do I get out of all this?

Your life. Oh, wait, I didn't tell you what would happen if the Midnight Man caught you, did I?

He rips your organs out and you die.

Have fun!

REECE

Where was everyone?

Reece paced around the assembly hall. The circle of salt was still there, but the girls were nowhere to be seen. He'd thought about going to look for the fit one but had decided against it. He'd wait for the rest of them to show up here and finish his sweets instead. He wouldn't have to share them that way.

He walked the perimeter of the hall slowly, watching his candle and chewing on the last few cola bottles which were warm from his pocket. You could tell it had been proper posh in here once, but the paint was scuffed and needed a touch-up, plus there were Jesus selfies *everywhere*. The walls were panelled with wood until about hip height, but that was mostly hidden by hulking old radiators that stood sentry every few paces. Reece knew just by looking at them that they were probably turned off in the winter and boiling in the summer. A large white projector screen dangled from the ceiling at one end of the room, practically glowing now he had got close to it, and Reece made his way over. A string with a metal loop tied to the end dangled from it.

He couldn't help himself.

Reece leaned forwards and hooked his finger through the loop, tugging at the string. It didn't budge, so he let go and was almost whipped in the face as the screen was sucked back into the ceiling.

"Whoa." He said it louder than he wanted to, his heart pounding as his voice bounced around the wood panelling. An acrid smell tickled his nostrils. Something was burning. No, not burning.

Smoking.

"Aw, man." The gust of the wind from the screen had taken out his candle flame. The candle was a short, fat one he'd found at home, one of several his mum kept in a weird little alcove where a fireplace had once been. She hardly ever lit them and the whole thing seemed pointless to Reece, but they had come in handy tonight. He headed towards a podium he'd spotted next to the projector screen, the only place he could rest his candle apart from the floor. The stand was full of clutter, along with an ancient laptop and a cold, half-full mug of tea, but there was just enough room to rest his candle. He placed it carefully in a space next to the milky – and, he noticed, slightly mouldy – brew. He resisted the urge to push the edges of the candle so it would let the molten wax run free down the sides. Instead, he grabbed the matches from his pocket and lit the wick with seconds to spare. He was pretty sure none of this Midnight Man stuff was real, but it didn't hurt to keep it lit, did it? Look what had happened to Mei when her candle wouldn't relight.

He started pacing again. This side of the hall was lined with curtains, and he ran his hand along the scratchy fabric, looking for an edge to hold on to. When his fingers closed around a hem he kept walking, dragging it along behind him, the track at the top squeaking slightly. It was heavy and soon caught, sticking in place. Reece started to let go, but before he did, he glanced back and was faced with his warped reflection in the darkened window. It didn't quite look like him – his eye sockets were a little too dark, his skin a little too grey.

"Reece?" A shudder ran through him and he dropped the curtain involuntarily, starting at the sound of his name in the dark. "Are you there?"

The voice was hoarse and he couldn't place whether it was male or female, never mind which one of those dweebs it was. He could tell that it seemed to be coming from outside the hall, though.

Should he move?

What if he didn't want to?

"Is someone up there? Mei?" The voice was louder now, coming closer to the hall. Reece squared his shoulders and thrust his chest forward, making himself look as big as possible in his baggy black T-shirt.

"Hello?" he called. Hello, was that all he could think of? He saw his candle flicker slightly out of the corner of his eye.

"Reece?" The voice sounded more familiar now and Ellie appeared in the doorway, panting a little as she dropped a bag to the floor but still as gorgeous as he remembered. "Thank God it's just you. Did you give Mei a candle?" Ellie caught sight of the empty salt circle. "What the hell, Reece? Where's Mei?"

"I dunno," he admitted. She was pretty and everything, but he was starting to think she had a bit of an attitude problem. "You were the one who was meant to be waiting with her."

Ellie's shoulders sagged. Her breathing was still strained, like she'd been power walking. "I know. Oh god, I only meant to leave her for a minute. I heard that scream and—"

"You heard a scream too?"

"Yeah. I thought it sounded like Toni, so I went to check it out. I *thought* she was in trouble." Ellie snorted softly.

"What does that mean?"

"Oh, nothing." She shook her hair out. "Wait, if you heard a scream, why didn't you come looking as well? Instead of hiding away in here?" she demanded, shouldering Mei's bag once more.

"I didn't hear it; Callum did. He swore he'd heard a scream. We were out in the hut, though, plus I'm like, half deaf. I never heard anything."

"So did Callum go looking then?" Ellie walked over to the salt circle and took a candle from Mei's bag before placing it in the centre, as if it was waiting for her there.

"Dunno … I left him on the stairs. He said he was going to the library to check for Mei's bag, but I wanted to get back and, er, check on you guys. I've not seen him since."

Ellie faced him and frowned, one strap of her own bag slipping from her shoulder. "Callum wasn't in the library. I checked."

"But the bag was?"

"Yeah. Along with something else I wish I *hadn't* seen."

"What?" Reece lowered his voice. "Like Midnight Man stuff?"

"Er, not quite. Let's just say I know where Toni and Hugo have been, anyway."

"Oh." Reece's eyes widened. "Ohhhhhhh. Ew, really?"

"Mm-hm." Ellie wrinkled her nose. She was so close now that he could see the tiny beauty mark on her collarbone. "I mean, it was disgusting. They were properly going for it." One side of her mouth lifted in a smirk. "I guess it's not against the rules."

"Right." Was she coming on to him? She was standing so close to him now, but it was the only way they could see each other in this light. It didn't mean anything.

Did it?

She was saying something else now, but he couldn't focus on it. The candlelight was casting shadows on her white top, and Reece couldn't seem to peel his eyes away from her. He stared at her mouth. Screw it. He leaned forwards.

"What are you doing?" Ellie took a step back, cupping a hand around her candle to protect the flame. Reece paused, his mouth slightly open.

"Er…"

"Seriously? We're in a school that we *broke in to*, playing a ritual game that supposedly summons a *demon* and every person who identifies as male is thinking with their *trousers*." She pushed the fallen strap back on to her shoulder. "Unbelievable."

"I wasn't going to do anything!" Reece protested, rubbing the back of his neck and taking a step back. He'd misjudged that, then.

"Whatever." She stalked over to the door. "Come on, we need to find Mei, give her the spare candle and then look for Callum."

"You, er, want me to come with you?"

"Not particularly, but I'm not going anywhere on my own again." She stepped into the hallway. "Just keep your hands to yourself, please."

"Of course." Reece followed her out into the hallway, watching as she approached the doors that led back towards the art room. "Bitch," he whispered, not quite loud enough for her to hear.

 chat

Inbox (@WitchesBrew_2007)
>Direct message< 27/10/2021 14:27
From: Miss_contrary06

I got your Snapchat with the invite on, thank you. I'm sooooooo excited! I really need to get a costume now, though!

I shared the invite with @BANdit too, hope that's cool – we've had a few chats on here and I know he lives close by. He's pretty cute too, if his Snapchat profile is anything to go by. And if you like guys!

Outbox (@WitchesBrew_2007)
>Direct message< 27/10/2021 16:31

To: Miss_contrary06

Yay, glad you got it! And the more the merrier – I just want this party to be a success.

Not really into hooking up with people I've just met, so you can have him if you want, lol. In fact … I haven't really told anyone this, but there's someone coming to the party that I've kind of liked for ages. I'm planning to get a bit drunk and tell them how I feel … I think so, anyway.

Inbox (@WitchesBrew_2007)
>Direct message< 27/10/2021 16:50
From: Miss_contrary06

That is so cute!!! How perfect, you can start the game and then go and hide with them … in the dark … by candlelight. Perfect snogging scenario!

 chat

Going shopping for a costume this weekend, so I'll let you know what I get. I'm thinking … well, a skimpy something. Maybe Catwoman…

ELLIE

"Since when was this locked?" Ellie tugged at the round brass handle on the door that led into the art room. She knew it had been open before – they'd all stuck their heads in on the way past, hadn't they? It was the room with the clay pots on the windowsill and the box of junior hacksaws.

An involuntary shudder tickled her shoulder blades and she shivered.

"Dunno," Reece said. He was lounging against the wall opposite, decidedly cool since Ellie had turned down his advances. "It's a bit chilly now, innit? Come on, let's keep moving."

"Do you think she's in there? Maybe she locked herself

212

in or something?" Ellie rattled the door once more in frustration, but Reece remained silent. Ellie pressed her lips to the crack between the door and its frame. "Mei?" Her voice was muffled, barely audible, so she took a step back and pounded on the wood instead. "Mei!"

"You obviously need a key." Reece yawned behind her. "God, I'm knackered. Is this game done yet or what?"

"I wish," Ellie muttered, wracking her brain. Callum was the one who'd let them in, did that mean he had a full set of keys? None of the doors had been locked before and she was sure he'd said that he'd gone around unlocking everything before the game started. She pushed on the door once more. There was no chance they were getting in there without smashing it to bits and she wasn't even sure how they'd do that. They only had one choice. "We have to find Callum."

"Whatever." For a second Reece looked as though he wasn't going to move, but he peeled himself off the wall and followed Ellie towards the stairwell. The other classroom door was still open and she paused at it, calling Mei's name and listening for a response, but the room was empty. Silent.

"Here." Ellie pulled open the door to the stairs and held it for Reece, noting the goosebumps on his bare arms. "Wait, do you want to go back for your jacket? You just said you were cold, didn't you?"

"I'm fine, don't worry." He seemed to soften a little. "I

took it off and put it down somewhere. I'm always losing stuff. Thanks, though." He started to walk past her but hesitated. "Hey, I'm sorry about before. I thought you … you know. Sorry."

"Don't worry about it." The words came out more curtly than she'd intended, and she sighed, forcing her tone to match his. "Honestly, it's not an issue."

"OK."

They navigated their way down the dark steps in silence, their flickering candles and blind feet leading the way. They reached the central landing and were turning down the lower half of the staircase when Reece stopped. "Wait – I have a question."

"Hmm?"

"Do you think goth girl and posh boy are still going at it in the library?"

"Ugh," Ellie let out a tired bark of a laugh. "I hope not. I'm scarred enough from witnessing it the first time round. Who knows what they're up to by now?"

"I thought he liked you, anyway."

"Yeah," Ellie replied softly as they reached the bottom of the stairs, "me too." She stopped abruptly. "Wait. Did you hear that?"

"Hear what?"

"Shush." Ellie put a finger to her lips and strained her ears. There it was again. "That noise, it was like a groan. You didn't hear it?"

"Half deaf, remember?" Reece pointed to his ear.

"I'm sure I heard a moan." Ellie raised her voice. "Mei? Callum?"

"Ell … ie?" a deep, croaking voice sounded from inside the staircase and Ellie froze. How was that possible? She looked at Reece, eyes wide. He was as pale as she felt.

"I heard that," he said.

"Ellie? Reece?" The voice was clearer this time, though it was also thick and sleepy. Ellie held her candle out with a shaking hand and something glinted silver on the floor. She crept forwards and the keys came into focus, reflecting the flame in her hand a dozen tiny times.

"Callum?"

"Here."

Ellie inched closer to the sound of his voice, her candle now illuminating a large, dark alcove beneath the stairs. Piles of boxes containing multi-coloured exercise books were scattered around a body in the middle. "Callum! Oh God, are you OK? Reece, come and help me!"

"I think so." Callum had managed to push himself up to sitting and raised one hand gingerly to his head. "Christ, that hurts." He closed his eyes for a second, his skin ashy.

"What happened, mate?" Reece asked, crouching down next to Ellie. "And where's your candle gone?"

Callum's eyes popped open. "I don't know." He felt around on the floor, wincing with each movement. "I was walking up the stairs and I slipped so it … it went out. I tried to light it again but" – he held a hand up to his head again – "I can't remember anything else. I think someone hit me"

"Or the Midnight Man got you."

"Be serious, Reece," Ellie scolded. She looked down at the spare candle she'd been carrying for Mei and made a decision. She dug the matches out of her pocket and swiftly lit the candle, holding it out to Callum. "It was dark; you probably misjudged the stairs, slipped and hit your head, that's all."

"No, I think Reece is right." He took hold of Ellie's outstretched hand and crouch-walked out of the stairwell before unfolding to his full height, wincing once more, his eyes narrowing. "I think it's because my candle went out. This game is for real."

"So why aren't you dead? Why aren't your entrails hanging from the railing like birthday streamers? Hmm?" Ellie demanded, bending to pick up the keys. Callum held his hand out and Ellie dropped the heavy keyring into his hand.

"Thanks. I dunno, maybe because I got knocked out?" Callum said. "I guess it's no fun to play with someone who's unconscious. Thank God I still have these – I'd be in a world of trouble if I lost them."

"We need them; it's why we came looking for you. Mei has gone missing and the art room's locked. I think she might be in there."

"Did she get a new candle?" Callum asked, already climbing the first step back up. Ellie shook her head. "Come on, then."

They climbed the stairs as quickly as possible while keeping the candles lit. Ellie managed two at a time and they burst through the door at the top, practically on top of one another. Ellie watched impatiently as Callum muttered to himself, flipping through the keys.

"Oh, thank God you're here!" Ellie whipped her head up as Toni's voice echoed down the hallway. She didn't sound like her usual snide self and as they approached, Ellie saw her eyes were red and her brow was furrowed. "The art room door's locked and…"

"You think Mei's inside?" Ellie finished.

"Yeah." Toni nodded. "She's not in the hall."

Ellie grimaced. "Yeah, us too. Callum has the keys, though, we're going to open it up now."

"Thank goodness," Hugo mumbled from the darkness behind Toni. Well, look at that, the whole gang together again. Ellie thought of Mei. Well, almost. "We heard … moaning, I suppose."

"From in there?" Ellie asked.

"Yes." Hugo nodded. Oh God.

"Callum, you have to open that door, now!" Ellie got as close behind him as physically possible. He stood in front of the door, but his hands were visibly shaking as he tried each key in the lock.

"These ones aren't labelled," he apologized. Ellie could see sweat beading on his forehead and bit her lip in an effort not to shout at him. "They all look the same. I just have to keep … ah! Got it."

The door swung open effortlessly, as though it had been waiting for them all along. Ellie slid past Callum and stood in the doorway, her eyes searching the room for any sign of Mei. They finally landed on a dark figure at the far side of the room.

Ellie screamed.

28/10/2021   21:17

MindMannequin_X07: Hey, @WitchesBrew_2007, I went down a deeeeep rabbit hole about TMG last night. There are loads of posts on here from people who have "apparently" played (I think some of them are, like, creative writing exercises, maybe?) Could be fun to read and freak your party guests out with though?

21:20

WitchesBrew_2007: Oooh, I didn't think of that. Love how your dastardly mind works, @MindMannequin_X07...

BANdit: Links! I wanna read too.

Miss_contrary06: Saaaaame.

MindMannequin_X07: Two secs.

Grimilim: How's the party planning going, @WitchesBrew_2007? Did you get any further with the clean-up?

WitchesBrew_2007: Nah, not really. There's not much in there to be honest, but all the seats are still in the screening rooms, which is good. All we need to do is get there early on Saturday with the blankets and beers and stuff. I've bribed my big sister to get us booze and everyone's chipped in, so there should be loads.

Grimilim: Sounds awesome! Wish I wasn't at the other end of the country...

WitchesBrew_2007: Aww, I know.

MindMannequin_X07: Here. There's a couple. Last one is my favourite. I think it's definitely off Wattpad or somewhere, but it's tense AF. Enjoy!

MindMannequin_X07: www.deddit.com/d/ cantsleepwontsleep/donteffwiththemidnightman

MindMannequin_X07: www.deddit.com/d/ cantsleepwontsleep/followtherulesofTMG

MindMannequin_X07: www.deddit.com/d/ cantsleepwontsleep/soIplayedthemidnightgame

WitchesBrew_2007: Delightful bedtime reading, lol. Thanks!

WitchesBrew_2007: Also, why is it always the Midnight *Man*? Goddam patriarchy strikes again...

17/03/2017   04:43

ScaryAnna: I know it's late, but I'm not sure I'll ever be able to sleep again after tonight.

Allow me to explain.

A few friends and I decided to play The Midnight Game. I know, I know. Mistake number one. We live in college dorms (I'm in the US) and managed to convince everyone who lives in our block to play. We had a few beers and started the game at midnight, as per the instructions.

Nothing went right after that.

We tried our best to stick together, but that didn't last long. I was in the bathroom with my two best friends and, I swear to God, our candles all went out AT THE SAME TIME. It's a dorm bathroom, the kind you get between two bedrooms with a door on either side, so there isn't even a window in there. None of us could stop shaking enough to relight the candles all in time and one friend, let's call her Shelby, started freaking the fuck out. Like, seeing things in the mirrors and hearing voices from beyond the glass. She started crying like her heart was breaking and we had to drag her out of there, but she didn't want to go. She was trying to CLIMB INTO the fucking mirrors. We finally got her out of there and managed

221

to find everyone else. One of our other friends had a similar experience in the kitchen and he couldn't stop vomiting. He was curled in a little ball on the floor, retching and shivering like he had a fever of 104. It was some freaky shit, man, he was still crying when the others put him to bed.

Yes, we ended the game there and then. How could we not?

But that's why I'm still awake. I don't think we ended it properly, it was too early...

I mean, we did what we could. We blew out the candles and turned on the lights. We told the Midnight Man he wasn't welcome any more. But I don't think that was enough. I'm in bed now, in the room I share with Shelby, and every time I try to drift off to sleep, she makes this scared, whimpering sound. I've never heard a person make that noise before. I keep seeing shadows out of the corner of my eye, but no matter how fast I whip my head around, nothing is there.

And the voices.

They're faint, but they're really there. I can *hear* them. It's like something or someone just out of reach is calling to me.

And I can't stop thinking about those mirrors.

MEI

Dark shadows clouded Mei's vision. Making that bit of noise had drained what little energy she'd had left. She knew she was done now. Spent.

She had never really wondered what dying would be like; she was too young to even contemplate it, no matter how many spooky stories or ghost hunting shows she consumed. Death was for old people, sick people. Not for her.

How wrong she had been.

She hadn't realized, either, that you literally feel the life ebb out of you. She was frozen in her last position already, forced to listen to the spatter and drip of her own blood as it landed on the tiled floor beneath her. It had started as a gush, a rushing in her ears, but now the sounds were fading, the drips more sporadic. She had hoped at first that someone would come, someone would save her before she bled out. No, exsanguinated, that was a better word. But the door had been locked. She'd heard them outside, talking and rattling the handle before leaving. If only someone had just come to save her, she could have told them.

She wouldn't be able to tell them now.

Mei heard a scream as the shadows crept closer, but it sounded far away, like she was underwater. Like a mermaid, maybe. She wanted to close her eyes, to drift away peacefully, but her eyelids wouldn't cooperate. They were made of stone, fixed open and staring. Just before her vision faded completely, she saw that they had come after all. They had come to save her.

Mei took one final shallow breath. She tried to twitch her fingers, to loosen the piece of paper she held in them, but she hadn't been able to feel them for a while now. Even so, she kept trying. They needed to read it. They needed to *know*.

She wished she could tell them that the Midnight Man hadn't done this to her.

She wished she could tell them that one of *them* had.

 chat

---

Inbox (@Miss_contrary06)
>Direct message< 28/10/2021 22:04
From: BANdit
So? Are we crashing the party?

                Outbox (@Miss_contrary06)
                >Direct message< 28/10/2021 22:07

To: BANdit
Crashing? We're practically VIP guests. I'm even sending her costume ideas.

Inbox (@Miss_contrary06)
>Direct message< 28/10/2021 22:11
From: BANdit
So she bought it? She thinks you just want to go and hang out? Sweet.

                Outbox (@Miss_contrary06)
                >Direct message< 28/10/2021 22:15

To: BANdit
Hook, line and sinker. Like a lamb to the slaughter. Like a ... well, you get it.
You sure you're ready to do this?

 chat

Inbox (@Miss_contrary06)
>Direct message< 28/10/2021 22:18
From: BANdit
Sharpening my party favour as we speak.
Do you wanna meet early and go together?

Outbox (@Miss_contrary06)
>Direct message< 28/10/2021 22:21
To: BANdit
No, I think we should plan to arrive and leave separately, just in case.
Oh – and don't forget to delete this account before the party. You used a throwaway email, right?

Inbox (@Miss_contrary06)
>Direct message< 28/10/2021 22:29
From: BANdit
Of course. I'll delete this on the day, in case she changes plans or anything.

Outbox (@Miss_contrary06)
>Direct message< 28/10/2021 22:32
To: BANdit
Good shout. Remember, WhatsApp or Snap if you need me – they're encrypted apps. No Insta messages, OK?
Unless they're naughty 😊
See you Saturday.

CALLUM

Oh please no.

Ellie's screams faded as Callum's body involuntarily turned away from the scene in the art room. He heard, rather than felt, his knees hit the tiled floor as he started to take in huge gulps of air. His head was spinning.

"Mei! MEI!" Ellie was still screaming the girl's name, over and over, as though her words could thread the jagged edges of her neck back together again. Callum was staring at the floor, but the image of Mei's broken body was seared into his brain. He'd never unsee that.

"Oh God, oh, it's real. It's really happening. It's all real. Callum?" Toni's voice cut into his thoughts, and his head lifted in her direction, puppet-like, as though

227

he wasn't quite in charge of his own body. "Callum, your candle."

The room snapped back into laser focus. His candle was out. He leaned back on his heels and dug the matches out of his pocket, but every time he tried to open the box it slipped from his fingers and hit the ground. When had he started shaking so hard? He felt around in the dark, sucking in deep breaths, just like he'd told Mei to do before. Mei… His eyes lifted before he could stop them and the reality of her body splayed out on the table assaulted him once more.

He bit back a sob and finally managed to pluck a match from the floor, striking it weakly. Nothing. He tried again, monitoring his breath, and this time it sparked. He held it to the candle with one furiously shaking hand, praying that it would catch.

It did.

The flame seemed to give him courage and he climbed to his feet, though his knees felt like they were made of marshmallows. He avoided Mei and focused on Toni instead. She was huddled in the doorway next to Hugo, one hand hovering as though she was contemplating patting him on the back. An acrid smell drifted across the room and in the dim light, Callum could just make out that the poor guy had emptied his stomach on to the floor. He didn't blame him. He turned slowly, steeling himself for the inevitable scene.

Ellie was hunched over Mei. She had tried to stem

the bleeding. Stripes of Mei's blood decorated her legs and clothing, trails of dark, glistening red streaked across her forehead, marks from where she had moved her hair out of the way, he thought. She looked like some kind of ancient goddess standing over a human sacrifice. There was nothing she could do for Mei now. The other girl lay on her back where she had been pinned to the tabletop like an insect, her head hanging almost all the way off the edge. The back of Callum's throat burned as the contents of his stomach threatened to make a reappearance too. He was fairly sure the only thing keeping Mei's head in place at all was the vice that had been tightened around her slim neck.

"Who would do this?" Tears had made tracks in Ellie's make-up and black mascara lines melted into the blood on her cheeks. Callum gently placed a hand on her shoulder to guide her away, but she shrugged him off. She clasped Mei's open hand. "I'm so sorry. I should have been looking after you." She glanced at Callum. "She's so cold."

"So are you. Come on." He took her hand and pulled her towards the doorway. She gave in, following him, when he stood on something that made a metallic twanging noise. Callum looked down at the floor.

He'd stood on one of the junior hacksaws.

"What is that doing…" He stopped in the act of picking it up and retched. The blade was coated in coagulating blood, clots and scraps of skin between its teeth. "We need to get out of here."

"Wait." Ellie bent down carefully. Her candle illuminated a blood-stained roll of paper lying next to the small saw. She picked it up. "It must be Mei's. I'll keep it for her."

"Come on." Callum dragged Ellie out of the room, not caring if he was hurting her. Mei had been murdered. Callum's brain whirred. Mei had been murdered in the school his mum worked at, and she had been let in with the keys *he* had stolen. He was a mixed-race male from a working-class family who had broken into a school.

Where a *murder* had just happened.

He was going to go down for this.

"We need a plan," he mumbled.

"We *need* to ring the police," Hugo fired back at him. They were all in the corridor now and Callum pulled the door shut behind them.

"That's easy for you to say. You're white and you're loaded. Check your privilege, mate." Callum looked around the group. "All of you, actually. *I* was the one who let us in so I'm going to be the one who gets done for all this."

"You won't." He jumped as Ellie squeezed his hand briefly. "Reece and I can vouch for you. We were together, weren't we?" She looked around. "Hey. Where is Reece?"

"What?" Callum studied the group. She was right. There were only four of them.

"I don't think he came into the room, you know," Hugo said.

Toni shook her head. "No, he didn't. He was behind me, and I was behind Hugo. I forgot all about him when I saw ... and when Hugo was sick ... oh God."

"What do we do?" Callum asked. "I mean, we can hardly leave him on his own, can we? Look what happened to Mei. Her candle went out, she left the salt circle and ... and..." His voice gave out.

"We have to go and look for him," Ellie finished the sentence for him.

"I just want to get out of here," Hugo whined.

Callum clenched a fist in annoyance and forced himself to take a deep breath. Knocking Hugo out wouldn't help. Not in the long run, anyway.

"We have to finish the game," Toni whispered, her eyes on the art room door. "I don't want to risk ... whatever happened in there. Do you?"

Nobody answered.

"You know, I really don't feel so good," Ellie groaned. "I need some water." She looked down at the dark handprints on her shorts and winced. "And I need to wash ... all this ... off."

"We can go that way." Callum pointed back towards the hall and the foyer. "If we go straight through there's another stairwell at the end. It leads down to the staffroom and the toilets – you can get a drink and get cleaned up there."

"OK." Ellie pushed herself off the wall that appeared

231

to be holding her up and wobbled slightly. "Wait." The word came out thick and slurred. "I think I'm heading for a hyper."

"A what?" Toni squeaked. Callum glanced at her. All her bravado was gone, and she looked like a little girl playing dress up.

"Hyper. It's the opposite of a hypo. My blood sugar must be high. It happens sometimes if I'm stressed or … if I've had a shock." She took an open-mouthed breath. "I just need to check my bloods and correct. Then I'll be fine."

"Can you make it downstairs? Or do you need to do it here?" Callum asked. It wasn't ideal, but he couldn't cope with the only other rational person passing out. Not now.

All four of them looked back at the art room door.

"I can make it to the staffroom." Ellie started walking and Callum joined her, forcing himself not to run. Instead, he kept his head down, eyes on his flame.

"Follow me," he said.

29/10/2021   07:42

WitchesBrew_2007: Well, I don't know about you lot, but I read that last link and could NOT sleep last night! All the mirrors in my bedroom are going to stay covered for a while, I think.

08:03

MindMannequin_X07: Lol, sorry. Good morning, anyway. It was a great story though, right?

BANdit: What did I miss?

WitchesBrew_2007: Scroll back and check out those d/cantsleepwontsleep links. Some people have been taking this game *very* seriously.

BANdit: Awesome. I'll have a look later. It's gonna be so much fun. I can't wait to play.

MindMannequin_X07: What do you mean, *@BANdit*? You're planning on starting a game too?

WitchesBrew_2007: Yeah, with me! He's coming to the party with *@Miss_contrary06*. So excited to meet irl!

MindMannequin_X07: Oh, cool. Well, have fun guys!

MindMannequin_X07 left the chat

 chat

~~Inbox (@WitchesBrew_2007)~~
~~>Direct message request< 29/10/2021 08:15~~
From: MindMannequin_X07
Hey, sorry to private message you on here. I just wanted to say, please be careful meeting people off the internet. I know you're probably very sensible, but I just couldn't let it go without saying something. I'm leaving the thread now, but have fun (and be safe) at your Halloween party.

Message deleted by recipient.

TONI

"Almost there," Toni muttered as she crept behind Ellie, hoping the other girl didn't faint or something on the way down the stairs. They were almost at the bottom of the stairwell, and Toni couldn't tear her eyes from the fire escape. It was only a few steps away. What would happen if she just left now? Anything?

She was dying for a cigarette.

"Here." Callum held open the door into the corridor and Toni followed Ellie through it, Hugo at her heels. They were back near the staffroom again. She'd been here with Hugo, what – an hour ago? Not even that. It felt like a lifetime.

"Thanks." She tried to smile at Callum, but his face was

stony, eyes completely vacant. She didn't blame him. The scene upstairs had been something else. That girl's neck…

"I'm going to the toilet," Ellie announced, lurching towards a signposted room on their left. Toni hesitated, looking back at Callum and Hugo.

"Is she OK?" Hugo asked. His face was drawn tight, skin stretched over the bones beneath and his voice was small. She hadn't realized he hated blood until he'd heaved all over the floor. Toni shrugged.

"You'll have to go with her," Callum announced to Toni, snapping out of his funk. "We'll wait for you in the staffroom, get her a glass of water or something."

"I…"

"You'll be fine," Callum cajoled her. "We will be right across the corridor. The staffroom door is propped open, and you could probably do the same to the bathroom one if you wanted to. We'll be seconds away if you need us. OK?"

"OK," Toni repeated numbly. They were splitting up again, despite everything that had happened since the first time.

She wondered where Reece was.

"Ellie?" Toni pushed the bathroom door open and stepped into the dark space. It was decorated sparsely: the basic breezeblock walls painted a sickly yellow colour. Directly in front of her there were two small toilet cubicles, a small plastic set of drawers to the right and two sinks hanging on the wall to her left, one long mirror stretched across the wall above them. Ellie was standing in front of it, her candle held up to her face as she peered at herself.

"It's everywhere," she whispered. She was right. Toni stared at the blood smears on Ellie's face and drifted down to the finger marks on her legs. The frayed hems of her stonewashed denim shorts were splashed with rust and her frilly white top was ruined. Toni licked her lips, her mouth dry.

"I'm not sure we'll be able to get it out of your clothes, but we can clean your face up a bit." She put her own candle down on the little plastic drawers and pulled a wad of paper towels from a dispenser on the wall. She turned the tap on, and they both jumped as the water exploded into the sink, Ellie's candle flame wavering desperately. Toni wet the towels and held them out to her. "Here." She took the candle from Ellie's hand and placed it next to her own as the other girl gratefully accepted the sodden tissues.

"Thanks."

Toni watched her for a second. The blood had already started to dry in places, but a couple of thick black lumps came away on the towel as Ellie wiped her face. She swallowed her revulsion down.

"Hello?" There was a gentle knock on the door. Toni looked away from the bloody girl and tugged at the handle. "Is she OK?" asked Callum.

"I think so. She's not really with it."

"It's the shock, I think, and the hyper. She needs to sort her blood sugar out before she's no good to any of us. Here, give her this." Callum pushed his hand through the crack. A long black hoodie dangled from it. "She looks freezing; tell her to put it on."

"OK." Toni shut the door, wondering if any of the boys here would be handing over their jumpers to her if she looked cold. She looked back at Ellie, who was scrubbing at the specks of blood that decorated her clavicle. "How's it going?"

"It's useless." Ellie threw the paper towels into the sink in frustration. They were stained a browny-red colour and little rolls of wadded up paper dropped into the sink from where she had worn a hole in the towels with her scrubbing. Her face was red but looked much cleaner.

"You look a bit better. There's got to be something else we can use, though." Toni scanned the room. There, a first aid kit. "Here." She lifted the green plastic box off its mount on the back of the door and rested it on the sink. She popped the latch that kept it closed and rifled through the contents. "Plasters … bandages … safety pins … ah, here. Alcohol wipes." She pulled a white square packet free, ripped the top of it off and handed the wet sheet to Ellie. The sharp, clean smell of rubbing alcohol filled the little bathroom. "That should help with the … you know … on your legs."

"Thanks." Ellie pushed open the door to a cubicle, lowered the toilet lid and sat down heavily. "It's everywhere," she repeated.

"I know." Toni winced. The alcohol wipe devoured the blood stains and Ellie started rubbing at her shoulders again. "Here." Toni picked up Callum's forgotten jumper and handed it to Ellie. "Put this on. It'll cover the stains on your top until you can get home and burn it."

"Burn it?" Ellie looked up sharply. "It's evidence. Why would I burn it?"

"Oh, yeah, I guess it is. I just meant you won't want to wear it again."

"That's for sure." Ellie pushed her arms into the sleeves and ducked her head, pulling it down over her. The cuffs dangled past her fingertips so she had to push them up her forearms. She leaned on the toilet roll dispenser and stood up. The jumper covered her shorts almost completely, leaving just the frayed hems sticking out. "Bit big." The corner of her mouth twitched ever so slightly.

"Just a bit," Toni agreed. "You ready to go?" Ellie shook her head and lowered herself back to seated, wincing as though in pain.

"God, my head. No, I need to check my bloods. Hand me that bag?"

Toni picked up the tote from under the sink and passed it over. It was surprisingly heavy. "What have you got in here, bricks?"

"Coke," she mumbled, pawing through the contents, "and no, not that kind."

"Yeah, 'cause what we *really* need is to be high right now."

"Yeah." Ellie produced her little black wallet. "Keep talking, will you? It helps me focus."

"Um, sure." Toni faltered. "I don't know what to talk about."

"Tell me about your necklace." Ellie pointed at the slim silver chain around Toni's neck. "It's cute. I have a similar one; my best friend gave it to me. Who gave you yours?"

"Er, no one. It's a charity shop special." Toni reached up to hold the half of a heart that sat in the dip of her throat. "I just thought it was cool."

"It is. So, no one special in your life?" Ellie raised her eyebrows as she removed the cap with her teeth and pricked her finger.

"No, *grandma*," Toni snorted.

"Wha' abou' 'ugo?" she said, forcing her words out around the cap. Toni winced. "Oh, God. Really? That bad?" Ellie smeared her own blood across a little strip of card, just like she had in the hall earlier. "Fine, I won't ask any more."

"It's OK. It wasn't what it looked like, though."

"Well it *looked* like he was going to—"

"Yeah, I know." Toni held one hand up. "Trust me, I know. But…" She felt the corners of her mouth turn down as her eyes filled up. She tried to contain the sob as she continued. "He was going to try and ... you know. Well I think so, anyway." She sniffed, her eyes threatening to overspill now.

"And what?" Ellie narrowed her eyes, using one hand to insert the strip into the small machine she'd used earlier. "You didn't want him to?"

Toni didn't reply, letting the tears drip down her face.

"Oh, hell no," Ellie growled, pushing herself to her feet. "He's a dead man."

 chat

You ABSOLUTE idiot. Why did you have to let it slip on that thread that you were playing that stupid EFFING game. Jesus!
We're going to have to delete these accounts early now, you know that?

Calm down. No one thought anything of it, and it's not like any of them know who we really are. They don't care.
Anyway, she's the one that dobbed us in and said we were going to her stupid party.

Only because you opened your big mouth. What if someone gets suspicious?

Of what? We've planned it too well. The whole thing is just going to

look like a tragic accident. Plus, one of those losers has already left
the thread — they won't have access to anything any more.

Outbox (@Miss_contrary06)
>Direct message< 29/10/2021 12:24
To: BANdit

Are you sure? You know I'm just looking out for us, don't you, baby?
We're way too pretty for prison…

Inbox (@Miss_contrary06)
>Direct message< 29/10/2021 12:25
From: BANdit
I'm sure. And I know you're doing your best.
Let's change the subject.
What are you wearing?

Outbox (@Miss_contrary06)
>Direct message< 29/10/2021 12:25
To: BANdit

What, now?

Inbox (@Miss_contrary06)
>Direct message< 29/10/2021 12:26
From: BANdit
Well no, but…
I meant to the party. What's your costume?

 chat

Outbox (@Miss_contrary06)
>Direct message< 29/10/2021 12:27
To: BANdit

Oh! Ha. It's … tight. Mainly latex.

Inbox (@Miss_contrary06)
>Direct message< 29/10/2021 12:28
From: BANdit
Wipe clean, practical…
Easy access?

Outbox (@Miss_contrary06)
>Direct message< 29/10/2021 12:28
To: BANdit

Niiiice.
But yeah, I think it is.
What about your costume? You know you need to hide your face,
right? Mine has a mask.

Inbox (@Miss_contrary06)
>Direct message< 29/10/2021 12:29
From: BANdit
Yeah, of course I know.
I'm going old school. Got one of those black and white ghost face
masks.

 chat

Outbox (@Miss_contrary06)
>Direct message< 29/10/2021 12:29
To: BANdit

Perfect. Right, I'm deleting this account now. Make sure you do the same!
See you tomorrow, babe.

Inbox (@Miss_contrary06)
>Direct message< 29/10/2021 12:30
From: BANdit
I'll delete it now.
See you tomorrow…

HUGO

"What do you think is taking so long in there?" Hugo paced the staffroom as quickly as his candle would allow. He'd messed up in so many ways tonight; he couldn't get his thoughts straight. Walking always helped.

"I dunno, man. Hey, stop that, will you? You're making me anxious." Callum's thin frame slouched against a tall cabinet door in the kitchen area. He looked even skinnier now that he'd taken his hoodie off.

Hugo stopped in front of him. "I reckon we're all pretty anxious, don't you?" He tried not to think about it, but the spectre of Mei's pale, bloodless form was seared into his eyelids. "Do you … do you think he did it?"

"He who?" Callum rasped. He sounded exhausted. "He as in Reece? Or he as in the Midnight Man?"

Both boys' eyes moved to Hugo's candle as the flame flickered.

"I don't know," Hugo whispered. "I just know I want to get out of here."

"I bet you do, you absolute pervert." Hugo snapped his head up to see Ellie fill the staffroom doorway. Her eyes were narrowed at him in fury and in the glow of the candle he could just make out Toni's mascara-streaked face in the hallway behind her. "How dare you."

"Whoa, I'm sorry," Hugo stuttered, taking a step back. "I didn't think you'd care. I know I shouldn't have kissed her; it was entirely inappropriate and…"

"Inappropriate?" Ellie bellowed, following him into the room. Hugo swivelled his head to Callum for moral support, but the other boy didn't move a muscle. "You call sexually assaulting someone *inappropriate*?"

"What? No! I didn't, I mean, I would never do that again…" Hugo clamped his mouth shut as Callum pushed up to his full height.

"What did you say?"

"No, no, listen…" Hugo's words fell out of his mouth in a tumbled panic. "I did not assault anyone, OK? She started it." He pointed a shaking finger at Toni, who was now hunched in the doorway, silent tears streaming down her face. "She came on to me."

"Just because someone initiates something doesn't mean you have carte blanche to do whatever you want to them!" Ellie yelled at him, her voice absurdly loud in the empty building.

"But you wanted to, didn't you?" Hugo stared at Toni. Her eyes were red from crying and long, grey stains decorated her cheeks. "Didn't you?"

Toni didn't answer.

Hugo clenched his free fist, eyes darting between his three companions. There was no way he was going through this again, he couldn't. He had been so careful this time.

"Why did you say *again*?" Callum's voice was low and in the darkness his eyes were pools of black. Soulless.

"I … I didn't." Hugo took another step back and his legs hit a low coffee table. He inched around it, putting the piece of furniture between himself and the others.

"Yes, you did," Ellie said, her voice flat. The three of them moved towards him in the blink of an eye, quick, jerky movements that didn't seem quite human.

"Stop!" Hugo pushed his free arm out, as if that would stop them, and blinked furiously. They weren't as close as he thought, his mind must be playing tricks on him. He needed to get out of this hellhole.

"Wait." Callum tipped his head to one side. "I think I know who you are." Hugo shook his head furiously. "You're that kid who got away with assault." He looked over at the girls as Hugo felt the blood drain from his face and his mouth filled with cotton. "Some guy from that boys' school in Heaton was arrested after he assaulted a girl from my school. She had to testify in court and everything, but the guy got off with a suspended sentence." He turned to face Hugo, his face a mask of disgust. "She was friends with my mate's sister. She failed her exams after that, didn't get into college. You screwed her life right up."

"I didn't *assault* her." Hugo's voice was small, but they all heard him. "She … she was up for it, honestly. I just…" He sucked in a deep breath. "I just didn't realize she'd fallen asleep." The words stuck in his throat, but he pushed himself to continue. A last confession, maybe. "We were so drunk, and I didn't … I didn't think about the consent. I thought it was implied, but I know better now, really, I do. Once I realized she was unconscious I stopped, I promise," he finished.

"You thought it was implied?" Ellie's eyes grew wide, and she took a step back. Hugo wasn't sure if it was physical repulsion or an effort to protect Toni, who clung to the door frame like it was a life raft. "I don't believe this." She raked a hand through her snarled hair and Hugo noticed that bloody streaks still decorated the underside of her arm. "You know what? Screw you and your toxic masculinity. Someone has been killed. We need to find Reece and get out of here before someone else is. Then I never want to see any of you ever again." She started to sob. "What the hell was I thinking?"

"Shush, princess, you're OK." Four pairs of eyes turned to the opposite end of the room where a door now stood open. Hugo hadn't even realized that there was another entrance to the staffroom, but sure enough a tall dark figure stood there, a candle in his hand. Reece. He took several quick strides into the staffroom and pain exploded in Hugo's face as he dropped to his knees, dazed. "Miss me?"

Hugo tried to take a deep breath, hoping it would calm the starbursts that were dancing in his vision. His mouth tasted sharp and metallic, and it took him a second to realize that Reece stood over him, rubbing the fist that had just broken his nose. Hugo coughed, choking on his own blood streaming down the back of his throat as he tried to climb to his feet. His head was fuzzy, and he could hear the others shouting, though they sounded far away. He wiped a hand across his face and his dizziness increased tenfold when it came back warm and soaked with red.

"What the hell, Reece?" Hugo was hauled roughly to his feet and Callum shoved a tea towel at him. "Here, stop the bleeding with this." Callum grabbed Hugo's hand – *wait, where had his candle gone?* – and forced his fingers to pinch the bridge of his own nose. "Sit down," Callum commanded and Hugo dropped on to a lumpy sofa.

"Can-ul," he gasped between deep breaths from his mouth, but Callum ignored him, squaring up to Reece.

"I heard everything," Reece spat. "He's a scumbag who

attacked Toni. He probably killed Mei too. We should do him in."

"Stop it!" Ellie yelled. Hugo tried to raise his head at the sound of her voice, but pain bloomed through his skull, so instead he settled for watching Ellie's feet as they pushed between Callum and Reece's. "Just stop. Let's get back to the hut and wait this stupid game out, then go our separate ways. We can make an anonymous call to the police about Mei." Ellie's voice cracked on the name. "Get him up and let's get out of here."

"I'll do it." Hugo heard Callum say. He watched Ellie's feet move back towards the door as Callum grabbed his arm. "Come on," he muttered.

"One second," Reece said.

Hugo squinted up as Callum was pushed out of the way.

"What are you—" Hugo's words were cut off as his head was yanked back hard, cold fingers wrapped in his hair. Hugo tried to twist out of the other boy's grip, but Reece was strong. He glared down at him, a manic gleam in his eyes.

"I'm not done here."

30/10/2021   16:52

Grimilim: Hey, @WitchesBrew_2007, ~~@Miss_contrary06~~ and ~~@BANdit~~! Have fun at your party tonight! Gutted I'm so far away. Maybe we can make it happen next year!

WitchesBrew_2007: Thank you! And yeah, for sure. I'll report back tomorrow. I'm heading out soon.

Grimilim: I tried to tag the others, but it wouldn't let me, must be a weird glitch. Tell them I said hey!

WitchesBrew_2007: Will do. See ya!

31/10/2021   02:53

WitchesBrew_2007: Is anyone there? @Grimilim?

31/10/2021   02:55

WitchesBrew_2007: Please?

WitchesBrew_2007: I'm scared.

WitchesBrew_2007: I feel ridiculous doing this, like I'm writing Midnight Game fan fic or something. But I'm alone and I don't know if I'll make it past 3:33 a.m., so I feel like I need to get this out.

Just in case.

For anyone who reads this, I'm at a Halloween party in the old Mayfair cinema, the derelict building off Clarendon Old Road. I've barricaded myself into what I think is an old cleaning cupboard, close to the main entrance. As soon as the clock turns 3:33 a.m. I'm getting the hell out of here.

We started just before the clock struck twelve and everything seemed fine – at the start. Sorry, my thoughts are all over the place and it's cold – my hands are shaking with the effort of trying to type this coherently. I know what you're going to say. It's not *real*; it's just a *game*. No one has ever really been killed playing it, have they? Well, I don't know and I sure as hell hope I don't find out. All I know is shit got really weird and everyone disappeared. Just – poof. Gone. I was stuck in this eerie old place on my own, and I didn't know what to do. Have you ever spent the night in an old building? There are noises everywhere and I don't know if they're being made by birds, rats, people … or him.

The Midnight Man.

I know the rules say no phones, but I was getting fed up of pacing the building and crying until I felt sick. Tonight was meant to be fun. Instead, it's turned into my own personal horror movie. I don't know if this game is real or not, but I thought the best thing to do would be to lock myself away until it's safe to leave. And I can't leave until 3:33 a.m. because … well, just in case it *is* all real. If you leave the building, you die.

I know I'm not making sense, but let me try to explain. I stashed my stuff in this cupboard when we arrived. I met friends, we drank, danced … someone brought speakers and everyone came in costume. It was awesome. I took some photos, but I don't think I should post them anywhere yet – I have a feeling I'm in enough trouble as it is. So, anyway, the night went as planned until it was time to play. Only a few people wanted in – some had hooked up on the old velvet seats and others had drunk too much. Some people started drifting home, others were calling taxis and heading into town.

That just left three of us.

I was a bit disappointed to be honest. Only my *new* friends had stuck around – my best friend didn't even make it to the party. I know it wasn't her fault, but still. I could really do with her right now. Anyway, they had read all the same stuff as me online, so we knew what to do. I think it was around 1:00 a.m. when I lost them. There were these noises, you see, like I mentioned before. Only, when you're in the middle of the game, you don't know if those noises are innocent. Or not.

When they decided to check out the sound, I went after them, but they turned a corner and then they were gone. I can't tag them any more either, I don't know why, but guys, if you read this, please come and find me. I'm in the cleaning cupboard near the main entrance. The door has a little window in it.

31/10/2021   03:16

WitchesBrew_2007: Oh God, why did I write where I was? I'm sure there's a dark figure at the window, but I'm too scared to move. I don't know where the others are, and I'm not about to go looking for them, so I've raided my bag and pulled out every single tea light I had stashed in there. They're all lit now, and I've emptied the contents of a huge tin of salt too so I'm surrounded by a thick band of white. I can taste it when I lick my lips.

Just over fifteen minutes to go. I can do this. I'll get out and order an Uber to take me straight home, then I'll call L. She'll know what to do.

31/10/2021   03:21

WitchesBrew_2007: There's definitely something at the door. I keep hearing my name being rasped through the wood, but I've had so much to drink I'm not sure if I'm imagining it or not.

God I hope I'm imagining it.

31/10/2021 03:25

WitchesBrew_2007: @*Grimilim*? ANYBODY?

31/10/2021 03:27

WitchesBrew_2007: Oh, God, I'm so sorry. I think I'm going to die, and I'm so sorry for all the times I've been horrible.

31/10/2021 03:28

WitchesBrew_2007: Mummy. Mum … I love you. I'm so sorry. Say bye to Daddy for me. Tell Melissa I'm sorry I wasn't a better sister. I love you all so much.

31/10/2021 03:29

WitchesBrew_2007: L. I'm so glad you couldn't come now. I'm so glad you're safe.

WitchesBrew_2007: I need to tell you something, though, before I go. Don't freak out.

31/10/2021 03:31

WitchesBrew_2007: I think I'm in love with you. I'm so sorry.

WitchesBrew_2007: I'm so sor

31/10/2021   09:02

Grimilim: Hey, @WitchesBrew_2007, you OK?

31/10/2021   09:05

Grimilim: Hello? Let me know you're OK. You had me going there!

03/11/2021   15:42

@Grimilim left the chat.

REECE

Reece gripped Hugo's hair so hard he felt the product in it melt between his fingers.

"Stop it," Callum insisted, tugging at his arm, but his grip was too strong. Reece set his candle down on the table, not caring if it stayed lit or not, and reached into his trouser pocket.

"I spent ages on this," he said, rolling the yellow pencil between his fingers, bringing the point into Hugo's eyeline. "Found one of those electric sharpeners. Look how pointy it is." He laughed as Hugo tried to suck in a deep breath. "I saw this in a movie once – always wanted to try it." Reece placed the end of the pencil flat on the table and tightened his grip on Hugo's hair.

"Stop messing, man. He's had enough." There was a note of panic in Callum's voice, but the other boy didn't move. It sent a thrill of anticipation down Reece's spine.

"He just needs a scare." Reece tightened his grip. It was pathetically easy, like the other boy had frozen. "No fight or flight in this lad, hey?" he crooned, snapping his own head up to the girls. "A little help over here?"

"No!" Ellie's shrill screech made the others jump as she tore through the room and barrelled towards them, candle all but forgotten. Reece took the opportunity to hold the pencil still and shoved Hugo's face forwards. A high-pitched scream erupted from the other boy as his body began to buck and roil beneath Reece.

"What have you done?" Callum lay on the floor beside them, his arms around Ellie, who was wrapped in a tangle of arms and legs. Interesting. Had Callum been trying to protect her? Or was he holding her back? Maybe he had wanted Reece to punish Hugo after all.

"Pipe down," Reece snarled, yanking Hugo's head back as the other boy's screams faded to a whimper. Reece frowned. "I guess the internet was wrong. You *can't* kill someone with a pencil to the eye." Beneath him Hugo went still. Reece dropped the pencil and wiped his hands on his black T-shirt before he put two fingers to an unconscious Hugo's neck and shrugged. "Definitely not dead. Oh, well." He wagged his finger at Ellie and

Callum, still wrapped up in one another on the floor. "Don't believe everything you read, folks."

"Reece ... I ... oh my God." Ellie choked.

Reece looked down at the pretty girl and sighed. Such a waste. "Duh," he said in exasperation, wiping the blood off his hands again. God, this stuff got everywhere. He'd already lost a jacket, now he'd have to throw the whole tracksuit away. "Who else did you think it was?" He waggled his fingers around and dropped his voice. "The Midnight Man?"

"Guys?" Reece whipped his head around to see Toni still hovering in the doorway. He'd wondered where she had got to. "I ... I have a bad feeling."

"No shit." Callum jumped to his feet in one fluid motion and dragged Ellie with him. Reece tensed. This kid was looking for a fight.

"Listen to me," Toni said, looking down at the candle in her hand – even from across the room Reece could see it was flickering. "Where are your candles?"

"I dropped mine," Ellie said weakly.

"Me too," Callum admitted.

Reece felt a laugh start to rumble through his body. "Candles? You don't need candles, you idiots." He reached into his pocket and pulled out a smooth, metal object. It was heavy in his hand, the weight pleasingly distributed. He pushed a button, forcing the blade to spring out with a soft hiss of air. He twisted it in front of him, admiring the sharpened edge and caught a glimpse of his own dark eye in the polished metal. "There is no game here, no bogeyman." He lowered the knife and grabbed Hugo by the hair again. The other boy stirred. "Unless you mean me." Reece pressed the knife into Hugo's neck and pulled it across his throat in one swift motion. Callum and Ellie dived towards him, but it was too late – Reece watched as floods of dark liquid flowed down Hugo's chest. His eyes fluttered open, his hands reaching for his neck as Callum's body slammed into Reece's, knocking him off balance.

"Stay down," Callum warned him. The skinny boy was stronger than he looked. He straddled Reece and wrestled his arms over his head, smashing his arm into the floor once, twice. Reece leaned up and screamed into his face, but he couldn't stop him. Reece's fingers unfurled and the knife clattered to the floor where Callum picked it up and threw it behind him like it was on fire. "Toni! Grab the knife!"

"Callum, you have to help me!" Ellie squealed. Reece allowed his head to roll to the side as he relaxed a little. Ellie was crouched down in front of Hugo, her hands pressed to his neck, but it was no good. His once pale polo shirt was saturated now, and his eyes had glazed over. Ellie seemed oblivious to the blood that pumped beneath her hands. She was covered in bright red arterial spray. "I can't stop the bleeding!"

"Toni!" Callum barked, craning his head around.

"Help Ellie for God's sake! Or see if there's a phone; we need an ambulance!" Reece studied Callum as he glanced around the room. Reece reckoned he was looking for something to tie him up with. His grip loosened a little and Reece tensed, ready to make a move when a dull thud made him look up instead.

Ellie lay sprawled on the floor in front of Hugo. Toni stood over them both, smiling. She lifted the small, wooden bat in her hand and rested it on her shoulder.

"I don't know about you guys, but I've wanted to do that all night."

Reece only took a second to enjoy the moment of shock on Callum's face, before he gathered his strength and pushed the other boy off him. He used Callum's own weight to tip him off balance and then pulled his arms behind his back. Toni lunged, smashing the blade of Reece's pocketknife between Callum's ribs. The blow sent Callum to his knees and Reece let him drop, leaning over to kiss Toni on the cheek.

"Hey, babe." He smiled. "Welcome to the party."

 chat

>Direct message< 02/11/2021 20:47

To: HotDog45

Hey babe, got your snap. This is my new username.

Inbox (@User3678)

>Direct message< 02/11/2021 20:52

From: HotDog45

Seen anything?

Outbox (@User3678)

>Direct message< 02/11/2021 20:53

To: HotDog45

No, you?

Inbox (@User3678)

>Direct message< 02/11/2021 20:54

From: HotDog45

No. Reckon we might be in the clear.

Wanna do it again?

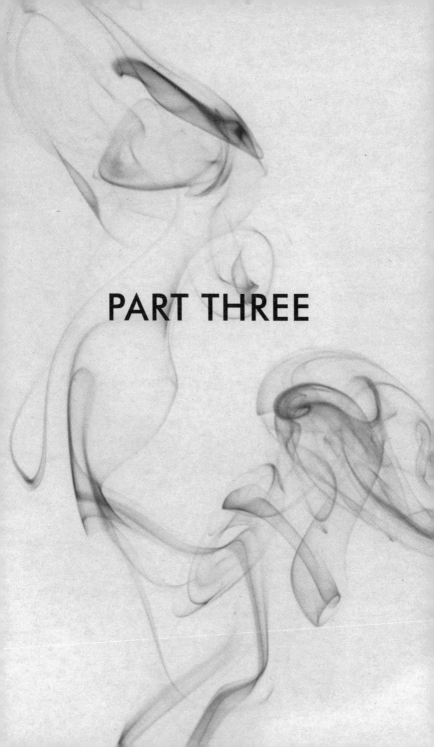

PART THREE

Friday 22nd October 2021

Al 15:57
Hey, are you coming to the park tonight?
You promised me you would!

> **L** 15:57
> I know I did, Al, but I dunno – I have to get this essay for psychology finished.
> Taking ages!
> Stupid Zimbardo and his stupid experiment.

Al 16:01
Ugh, I haven't even started that one yet. Just do it tomorrow.
On to more important things … what you wearing tonight?
We're discussing the Halloween party! You HAVE to come!

> **L** 16:03
> I've not even thought about it. It's so cold out. Might just strap my duvet to me.
> And I won't be able to write anything this weekend, I'm going away with Dad.
> You know what he's like. Enforced fun that was great when I was thirteen, not so much now.

Al 16:05

What, you mean he hasn't yet realized that day trips don't actually say "sorry for *shagging the neighbour*"?

L 16:09

Exactly.
Right, you have to leave me alone or I'll still be hanging out with weirdo Zimbardo rather than you later.

Al 16:10

OK, soz. Have fun, lol.
Oh – what time do you want me to meet you?

L 16:15

Half seven?
Will you meet me at the bus stop?

Al 16:23

Yeah, course.
Oh, and bring an umbrella. I left mine on the bus today.
Gutted.

L 16:30

Will do.
You know you're the only person I'd come out in the rain for, right?
My hair can't take the frizz.

Al 16:34

Yeah, yeah, I'm honoured.
Text when you're on the bus? I'll start walking to meet you then.

L 16:44

Of course. Love ya xo

Al 16:45

Love you too xo

ELLIE

Someone had sewn tiny little weights into her eyelids. At least, they must have done. Why else would she be struggling to open them?

"Insulin," she mumbled, though when the word came out of her mouth it was more of a slurring growl. Ellie gathered all the strength she could muster to peel her eyes apart, a dull pain in her head blurring her vision.

"Shhhh." A rough hand covered her mouth as she tried to scramble up from the floor. She didn't have the energy to scream, but her body flinched away instinctively. "It's OK; it's me. Callum," he wheezed. "They're in another room."

They? Ellie racked her brain to remember what had

happened as she turned to look at him. Callum lay on the sofa, his hands pressed to his side now. They were dark. Wet.

And then there was Hugo.

His body lay on the opposite side of the sofa, his head impossibly far back. His neck was open to the sky, his skin grey and waxy. Ellie's mouth filled with acid as she looked at her bloodstained hands and remembered clamping them to his throat. She turned her head as her body was racked by spasms, wanting to vomit, but there was little to throw up.

"Hey, hey, stop, please." Callum's eyes were pained. "I need you to wake up and get us the hell out of here. You've been out for, like, twenty minutes. I pretended to be out too, and they disappeared, but they'll come back if they hear us. I think … I think they want us to be awake."

"They?" Ellie rubbed the tender spot on the side of her head and winced. Had she been hit by something? Her temple was aching, bruised to the touch. She had to remember. "I can't think straight," she moaned, trying to keep her voice low. "I never treated my hyper. Toni distracted me and my moods get so out of kilter when my bloods aren't right."

"What do you need?"

"Insulin. If I don't do something now, I won't be good for anything." Ellie felt like she had drunk her body weight in alcohol, even though she hadn't. This hyper

271

was promising to be worse than that time she'd had her stomach pumped. She needed to treat it.

"They took our bags." Callum winced, trying to push himself up a little. "Can you have some sugar or something? I think there are biscuits over there. Just be quiet."

"No." Ellie shook her head, the throbbing pain making her suck air in through her teeth, regretting it immediately. "It's the opposite. My sugar's too high; I need to lower it." She lifted one arm gingerly and shoved it down beneath the frills of her crusted white top. "Help me, will you?"

"What?" Callum stared at her like she'd lost her mind, averting his eyes when she started to rummage around in her bra. "What are you doing?"

"Here," she said in quiet triumph. "You'd be amazed what a girl can carry around in her bra." She produced a small black cylinder and held it out to Callum.

"It's a tiny pen," he said flatly.

"It's a small insulin pen. It's my spare. Can you see that little dial at the bottom?" He squinted his eyes. Sure enough, there was a little window that had a zero in it, and a twisting mechanism at the bottom. "I think I was hit on the head, either that or this hyper is already sending me into shock. I can't see the numbers clearly."

"So, you want me to turn it?"

"Yeah." Ellie paused. Were there footsteps in the hallway? "Quickly," she lowered her voice. "Turn it to three, no, four to be sure. That should cover me for now."

"OK. I just have to do this." He winced as he lifted one hand away from his side and wiped it on his jeans. The coppery smell hit the back of Ellie's throat.

"You're hurt."

"Aren't you observant?" He held out his hand for the pen. "Tell you what, you hold it and I'll twist."

"OK."

They worked in silence for a moment, Ellie's eyes flitting between the two open doors. Reece could appear at any moment.

Reece. Her blood boiled. She knew she should be scared, but that wasn't the feeling that came out on top.

She was *furious*.

"There." Callum let go of the pen, and Ellie wasted no time removing the lid and slamming it into her thigh, a sigh of relief escaping her lips. "Is that it? Are you OK now?"

"It'll take a bit to work, but it's a start," she said, counting to ten before removing the needle, replacing the cap and sliding it back into her bra. "Now we need to find Toni and do something to sort you out." She squinted at Callum's T-shirt. "Did he stab you?"

"I was stabbed, yeah. Reece, no."

"What do you mean?"

"Reece didn't stab me," Callum said slowly. "Think about it – I had him on the floor while you were trying to help Hugo." His eyes drifted over to the other boy's lifeless form. Ellie shuddered. Thank God Hugo's eyes were looking the other way. She hadn't been able to save him, either.

"Yeah, I saw you struggle with the knife. I thought you got rid of it … you shouted for Toni… Wait." She touched the side of her head. "Someone *did* hit me." Callum nodded. "You were there." She pointed at the floor. "I was here, and Toni was…" Ellie drew a sharp breath. "Toni knocked me out?"

"With a rounders bat." Callum grimaced. "She laid you out cold."

"That little bitch," Ellie hissed. "I bet Hugo didn't even do anything to her, did he?"

"I dunno. You were the one she told."

Ellie cast her mind back to the discussion in the bathroom. "Er, I don't know if she did."

"What?"

"I don't know if she actually said anything. I think she got upset and I … kind of jumped to that conclusion?"

"Oh." Ellie couldn't tell what the look on Callum's face meant. "God, this is all so messed up."

"I know." Ellie felt in her pocket and pulled out the little piece of paper. "This wasn't Mei's secret, was it? It must have been Reece's. She was trying to warn us about him." She held it in the air and read aloud. "*'The reason I'm here: I want to kill again.'* Again? He's done this before?"

"He certainly seemed comfortable with that knife."

274

Callum wheezed. "Hey, what do you think Mei's reason was, then? Why was she here at all?"

"I think she had a lot of people to please." Ellie sighed. Poor Mei. "Maybe this was her way of acting out, having a little fun. Pressure can do weird things to people."

"Yeah." Callum glanced at Hugo. "Why do you think he was here?"

"I really don't know. Self-punishment, maybe? It sounded like he really was sorry for what he did." Ellie braved a look at the other boy. A small fleck of white stood out on his soaked polo shirt, just above the pocket. Ellie stood on wobbly legs and reached over to him as quickly as she could and plucked it out, avoiding the red gash at his neck. "Look."

"Is that his reason?" Callum asked.

Ellie unfolded the scrap of paper. "Yeah."

"What does it say?"

Ellie couldn't get the words out, so she held it out to him in silence.

"Oh." Callum took a shallow breath and Ellie looked down at the writing through teary eyes.

The reason I am here today: I need friends.

"Yeah." Ellie's blood boiled once more. "This is not going to happen to us, do you hear me?"

"I'm with you. What's the plan?"

"First of all, let's get the hell out of here. You need a hospital."

"But we can't leave until the game is over and it's only" – he squinted down at his wrist – "twenty minutes to three. We have almost an hour to go."

"You still believe in the game?" Ellie shook her head. "Everything that's happened has been because of people, Callum. They killed Mei and Hugo. If we don't get the hell out of here, we're next."

"I know."

"Plus, we've not had a candle for, what? Twenty minutes? And we've been fine." She looked down at the blood that covered them both and placed the tips of her fingers to her temple. "Well, you know what I mean."

"Maybe," Callum said. She rolled out her arms and her ankles, testing for injuries. Yes, she felt like she had the mother of all hangovers, between the rounders bat to the head and her bloods being all over the place, but she seemed otherwise unhurt. She stood up straight to stretch out her back and her foot crunched over something. She glanced down.

They were sitting in a huge ring of salt.

"Did you do this?" she asked.

"Yeah." Callum nodded. "When they left, I saw this huge tub on the table so I … well, I didn't see how it could hurt. I've been hearing weird noises, but I blamed it on the fact that I had massive blood loss and was stuck in a room with an unconscious girl and a dead guy. Anyone's mind would play tricks on them in that situation."

"Fair point." Ellie's eyes searched the kitchen worktops now. Biscuits, yes. Candles, no. "It looks like they've taken everything we had." She looked down at Callum. "They're going to be back any second – we need to make a choice. We either stay here and fight or we try to leave."

"What if we hide?"

"Hide? Sounds good to me. But where?"

"There's a little medical room off the main corridor just out there. There's one door in and one door out, on to the playground. We can lock ourselves in there. I didn't show it to anyone before and it kind of looks like a cupboard. They might not think to look inside."

Ellie sighed. "OK, but if we see them, we are running. Deal?" She looked at him. There was no way he could run in this state. "I'm assuming you don't have the keys any more?"

"No, Reece took them. But I know where the spares are. Over there." He nodded to the kitchen area. "On a hook under the sink. And check the bottom drawer – Mum calls it the junk drawer. There might be candles in there."

"OK."

Ellie placed her arms under Callum's armpits and helped ease him out of the chair. He stood up and instantly hunched over, a fresh trickle of blood cascading over his hands.

"Dizzy," he whispered, leaning against the arm of the sofa.

"Just stay there." Ellie raced to closest door, the one opposite the toilets, and peered into the corridor. She could hear voices. They seemed distant, but this place was essentially built as one huge circle. They could be coming from anywhere. "Which way to the medical room?" she hissed over her shoulder.

"Left." She eyed the distance to what looked like a cupboard door. Five metres away, maybe less? She could help carry him that far.

"Great." She retreated into the room and carefully inched the door under the sink open. A small row of hooks studded the back of it, each with a neat label above it. "God love your mother; these ones are all labelled."

"I know." Callum panted. "It's the … one that says … first aid."

"Got it." Ellie wrapped her fingers around the two keys that dangled from a green plastic fob to stop them clattering. She gently shut the door and turned to ease the bottom drawer open. It was packed with all sorts of rubbish, and there was no way she could have a good rummage without making a racket. "This one's not so organized." She let her eyes travel over the items she could see clearly, as Callum shuffled over behind her.

"There." He pointed. "Candles."

"Bingo." Ellie eased out a bag of small tea lights, before realizing they couldn't use them. "They're fake," she whispered, bending the plastic flame beneath her thumb.

"Safety candles," he groaned, "because, primary school. Do they work, at least?"

"Maybe." Ellie felt for the small switch on the bottom and flicked it. The plastic tea light gave off a merry, flickering glow. "Yep," she said, passing it to Callum, "that's working. We can take the bag, just in case." She pulled out another and flicked it on. It glowed in the dark. "I guess they'll have to do."

"OK. Can you help me?" Ellie nodded and Callum put the hand holding the candle around her shoulders, transferring some of his weight to her. Ellie's knees buckled a little, but she tensed her legs and straightened up.

"Got you. Oh, wait." She paused and bent her knees in order to pluck a roll of tape from the drawer, sliding it on to her wrist like a bracelet. "We can use this." She pushed the drawer closed with her foot before looking back at Hugo one final time. "I'm so sorry," she whispered to him.

"Come on." Callum began to shuffle to the door. "Let's get out of here."

Friday 22nd October 2021

Al 23:49
Hey, L.
You home yet?

L 23:51
Just.
I got the full on third degree from Mum.
She never believes me when I say I haven't been drinking.

Al 23:51
I think it might take her a while to get over the stomach pumping incident...

L 23:52
Yeah.

AL 23:52
Sorry, I know you don't like to be reminded.
Don't worry – she'll get over it eventually. And besides – I drink enough for both of us.

L 23:53
This is true.
So, are you psyched? For the Halloween party?

Al 23:54
YES.
It's gonna be EPIC.
You know Shauna Dawson's older brother,
Luke?

L 23:54
Kind of. He left college before we started,
right?

Al 23:55
That's the one.
Well, he's some kind of urban explorer now.
He's the one who suggested the old cinema.
Said it's still pretty put together in there.

L 23:56
That is so cool. And spooky.
Perfect for Halloween.

Al 23:56
Right?
Oooh, let's get everyone to wear a costume
from a horror movie!

L 23:56
Bagsy OG Scream.

Al 23:57

As if you're gonna wear a floor length robe. It would cover up the goodies.
You nearly froze to death tonight in that playsuit.

L 23:57

The goodies? You little perv ;)
I work hard for this peachy behind.
Anyway, not all of us are comfortable in head-to-toe black, my little witch.

Al 23:57

I'd be insulted, but I know you're a goth at heart. You just hide it behind pastels and a great blow-dry.

L 23:58

Why thank you.
Anyway, I meant I wanted my costume to be Tatum from the first Scream film.
That way I can wear a teeny outfit and just put a cat flap round my waist.

Al 23:58

Oh, bravo.
I love it.

L 23:58

What about you? Any ideas?

Al 23:59

I'm not sure yet.
Someone from The Craft, maybe?

L 23:59

Please tell me you mean the original Craft.
Not the one you made me watch last month
that *actually* ruined my life.

Al 23:59

It wasn't that bad!

Saturday 23rd October 2021

Al 00:00

OK, so it was.
Yeah, I'd have to do Nancy from the first one,
wouldn't I?

L 00:01

Yeah, that'll be easy.
Not far from your usual attire…

Al 00:01
Oi, be nice.
Oh, hey – did you like my present?

L 00:02
I LOOOOOVE it!
I've wrapped it around my wrist so it's a cute little double chain.

Al 00:03
Nice!
Did I tell you what happens when you put the broken hearts together?
It says "Best Witches" instead of best friends :)

L 00:04
You did.
You showed me.
Several times, in fact.
Nothing to do with that bottle of gin and lemonade...

Al 00:05
Ha.
Sorry.
You like it, though?

I told you, I love it.
I'm never taking it off.

L 00:05

CALLUM

The walk to the medical room seemed to take for ever to Callum. He felt like he was wading through mud: planting one leg in front and dragging the one on his injured side so he might stem the bleeding. All this while trying to keep one hand plastered to his wound and attempting to keep the majority of his weight off Ellie.

"We're almost there," she said through gritted teeth. They took two more slow steps and arrived in front of the door, its navy-blue paint shining in the weak candlelight. "Can you keep watch while I open it?"

"Yeah." Callum turned his head to look down the long, dark corridor as Ellie slid the key into the lock. "Nothing so far," he whispered. From here he could see down the corridor to the library, straight through the foyer, which was fairly bright as the streetlights from outside bled through the upstairs windows. All seemed still.

"Good. In you go." She eased the door open and pushed him inside. He sank gratefully on to the child-sized sickbed and sighed as she shut the door.

"Lock it," he said, realizing she was doing it anyway. She left the key in the door, the little fob dancing merrily as it hung there.

"Should I cover that?" Ellie pointed to a window fitted with patterned glass. A tiny desk was crammed beneath it, and it was next to the other door, which was about a foot away from the bed. The room was small, only really big enough for two people, and the only other bits of furniture were a tiny corner sink and a tall metal cupboard.

"Nah, it's privacy glass. Plus, it's looking over the playground. I think those guys are still inside."

"Right, well let me look at you."

"What do you mean?"

"We need to do something to treat that wound. How long do you think you'll be able to walk around holding your internal organs in using only one hand?" She moved over to the bed and sat carefully beside him. "Let me see."

"Get a first aid kit first." Callum gritted his teeth. "Or at least some paper towels?"

Ellie looked at the wall over the sink. "OK." She stood up and started pulling towels out, one-by-one.

"No – use the key. It's taped to the side of the dispenser."
He watched as Ellie felt around until she peeled away a
piece of masking tape. It was stuck to a flat piece of plastic.
"This?"

"Yeah. You see the prongs?" He thought about the
last time he had filled the dispensers for his mum. "There
should be two little holes on top of the casing. Press those
in and it'll pop open."

Ellie followed his instructions and sighed. "That's much
better," she said, easing the front of the dispenser down and
pulling out a wedge of paper towels. "Magic paper towels.
Did your teachers ever say that?" She put them on the bed
before taking two paper cups from a precarious tower and
filling them with water. "Drink."

She held the cup to his mouth, and he took several
small sips. "Thanks. Yeah, I forgot about that. Didn't
matter if you'd grazed your knee or broken your leg – the
answer was always 'let's put a wet paper towel on it'." He
chuckled, stopping short as he felt the edges of his wound
rub together. "Thanks." She put his cup down and drained
her own, filling it again and again. After she'd downed the
third cup, she put it in the sink and wiped her lips.

"Better?"

"Yeah. I'm always so thirsty when my bloods are high.
Right." She sat down again, holding the paper towels at
the ready. "There's a lot of blood, but it can't be fatal, can
it? Otherwise, you'd be … you know."

"I know."

"You let go and pull your shirt up. I'll press these on to stem any bleeding and then see if I can have a peek, OK?"

"Should I lie down? It's the only way I can think of to keep the bleeding above my heart. That's what you're meant to do, isn't it?"

"I don't know. I guess it makes sense?" Ellie chewed her lip and took a second to tuck her hair behind her ears as Callum manoeuvred himself on to his right side. He stared at the keys in the lock. "The key for the medical cupboard is on that keyring too. The first aid kits are in there."

"OK."

"Be quick," he begged. Callum began to inch up his shirt, a hiss escaping his lips. "I think she got me between the ribs, down near the bottom."

"OK," Ellie repeated. "Right – three, two, one, move!" Callum felt cold air pierce his side for a second and cried out before Ellie pushed the paper towels on to the wound, shushing him. "I'm so sorry; I know it must be agony, but you need to stay quiet."

Callum couldn't force out an answer.

"I'm going to take your belt off."

"What?" he said in alarm.

"You can bite down on it. It's what they do in gangster movies when a vet or someone is digging a bullet out of the bad guy. Unless you have a secret stash of whisky somewhere, this is all I can think of."

"Even if I did, I don't drink," he huffed, lifting his hips slightly as Ellie undid his buckle and pulled the belt out from the loops of his jeans.

"Me either," she said, handing him the belt. "So, you didn't drink from Hugo's flask earlier?"

"No, I pretended. You?"

"Same. It's basic girl code. I don't trust a drink I haven't poured myself."

"Sounds sensible." He bit down on the warm leather, trying to avoid the section that was soaked in his own blood. "Go," he said, voice muffled.

"I'll be as quick as I can."

He sucked in a breath as Ellie lifted the pressure on his side, biting down. It helped. He took deep breaths in through his nose which helped keep the darkness at the edge of his eyes away. If he let that creep in, he didn't know if he'd wake up again.

"I don't think it's that bad," she said as he felt the pressure resume on his ribs. "I mean, of course it's bad, you've just been shanked in the ribs, but the bleeding is slowing down and I think I can patch it up for now."

"Really?" He was starting to get light-headed now that the blood was getting back to his brain. It brought with it a strange sense of euphoria. He was going to be fine. Ellie would fix him, and they'd get out of here. He could go home.

"I can try. Here, press down on this." She closed his

hand over the paper towels and pushed off the bed. She slid the keys from the door and inserted the other one into the tall metal cabinet, swinging the doors open before replacing the key. "Bingo," she whispered.

Callum couldn't see the inside of the cupboard, but he'd helped restock it enough times to know where everything was. "There are two baskets on the top shelf – one of alcohol wipes and the other is little packets of gauze. Grab them and some medical tape from one of the green bags."

"This will work better." Ellie shook the duct tape on her wrist as she appeared in front of him, a basket in each hand. "Saw it—"

"In a movie?"

"Almost. On Deddit."

"Well, then it must be true." He saw the crestfallen look on her face. "I'm joking. I trust you. Well, as much as I can trust anyone at the moment."

"Fair." She sat down again. "I won't clean it. I don't know how deep it is and I don't want to aggravate it before you get to a hospital. I'll just put a stack of gauze over the gash, clean around it as best as I can and then tape over it. What do you think?"

"There's only one way to find out. Make sure you open loads of gauze first. And maybe have two piles – one for while you clean it and a fresh bunch to replace it before you tape me up."

"Good idea." They sat quietly for a couple of minutes.

The only sounds that Callum could hear were his own laboured breaths and Ellie tearing the paper covers from the gauze. "Where do you think they are?" Ellie asked quietly.

"I don't know. They said something about going for a smoke, so hopefully they've got high and forgotten all about us."

"I wish," Ellie muttered. "But we watched Reece kill Hugo and Toni stabbed you. They won't just leave without us. It's way too risky for them."

"Maybe. They left just before you woke up. I think they were getting bored of waiting for us."

"I think they'll be back soon. Right, I'm going to swap these for the gauze. You ready?" Callum bit down on the belt and nodded. "Well done. Press please."

"You have no idea how much this hurts," he grinded out between his teeth as he pushed on the thick pads. He tried to concentrate on the cooling sensation of the alcohol wipes that Ellie was mopping up his blood with instead.

"Sorry. I am trying to be gentle. I just want to get it all off so this tape will stick."

"I know," he grunted. She carried on, her touch feather-light but still sending a wave of pain through his body every time she touched him.

"Did it hurt?" Ellie asked. Callum could hear the caution in her voice.

"When she did it? Yeah. It's fine, I can talk about it."

"What did it feel like?"

"Honestly, I thought she'd punched me. It was like a really bad sucker punch to the ribs. It was only when she pulled the knife out and I started bleeding that I realized the bitch had stabbed me."

"I can't believe it." Ellie wafted a hand around to dry his skin off more quickly. The cool sensation was nice – it distracted from the pain a bit. "What are the chances of meeting two psychopaths on the internet?"

"*Folie à deux*." Callum remembered the phrase from the Slenderman stabbing conversation. "The madness of two. Maybe they were toying with us this whole time."

"Certainly seems like it."

Silence descended again as he watched Ellie methodically rip off lengths of duct tape and hang them from the edge of the desk. Callum felt the gauze start to dampen beneath his fingers. "I think it's time to change this. I'll sit up and when you swap it, just slap the tape all over. We can use the rest to wind around my ribs; if we do that tight enough it might stem the bleeding for a while."

"On it." She gently helped him into a more upright position and held out the fresh gauze. "Drop that one on three and press this on. I'll grab the tape. Ready?"

Callum nodded, clamping his teeth together.

"One … two … three!"

She shoved the gauze on and whipped a piece of tape from the desk, placing it over the lower part of the dressing. Callum tried not to move as she quickly slapped the rest of the pieces around it, forming an abstract little square on his side. "I'm going to put the end of the tape over the middle of the gauze and just … wrap, I guess." Callum raised his free hand in the air, focusing on the candles as Ellie passed the thick black tape from one side of his body to the other, then around his back, repeating the motion over and over. The candles continued to flicker merrily, completely unaware of the danger they were in. "Almost done," she breathed.

He nearly smiled – the last time he'd been wrapped up like this was for Halloween when he was nine and obsessed with ancient Egypt.

"You're done," Ellie panted, dropping on to the bed. "How does it feel?"

"Tight." He huffed as she rooted in a first aid kit. She produced a pair of round-edged scissors and cut the end of the tape away from the roll.

"Too tight?"

"No, fine." He flexed his arm experimentally. "It feels a bit better, thanks."

"Good." She started to pack the items back into the cupboard. "Hey, there's some pain relief in here."

"What?" Callum almost wept with joy. "Gimme."

Ellie handed him a bottle of Calpol.

"Are you serious?" he asked.

"It says it contains paracetamol." She shrugged, popping

the safety cap and holding out the sticky brown bottle. Even though the glass was dark, Callum could see it was almost full. "Beggars can't be choosers. Do you want it or not?"

"Of course I do." He took the bottle and pressed it to his lips, gulping greedily. "I think that's just pure sugar," he said once he'd drained it.

"Er, I don't know if you're meant to drink a whole bottle."

"Come back to me on that when you've been stabbed."

"Fair comment." Ellie cracked a smile. She stood on her tiptoes to place the baskets back on to the top shelf when she stopped to look at her watch. "Hey, it's just gone three a.m. We only have half an hour left."

"Seriously?" The muscles that had been knotted in his shoulders relaxed slightly.

"Yeah." She sat next to him, tidying the empty packages into little piles ready for the bin. His mum would appreciate that about her. "So, what is your excuse then?" she asked. "For not drinking, I mean."

"I guess it's because—" Callum was cut off by a bloodcurdling yell that echoed down the corridor outside. He froze, listening to what sounded like the staffroom being smashed to pieces.

"They're back," Ellie whispered. She closed the cupboard and leaned against it. "What do we do?"

"Is the door still locked?" Ellie nodded, but a look of uncertainty flittered across her face. "Is it?"

"I think s—" she clapped a grimy hand over her mouth as the handle started to turn. She stared at it with wide eyes and Callum could think of nothing else to do.

So he prayed.

"*O Allah,*" he whispered as low as he possibly could, "*Allah, stand by us. Allah, protect us.*"

"They can't be in there." Toni's impatient voice bled through the door. "It's locked and we have the key. We should try upstairs."

"Don't tell me what to do." Callum heard Reece snarl as the handle pushed lower. He held his breath as Ellie stared at him with wide eyes, but the door held and the lever was released. Ellie visibly deflated. "Fine. How far could they have got anyway? We took her insulin and you knifed him right between the ribs. I reckon you might even have got a lung." Reece laughed.

"Precisely," Toni said. Callum heard what sounded like the smack of a kiss and felt bile rise in his throat. "Besides, what are the odds we'd find our latest victims in a cleaning cupboard? It's not going to be *exactly* like last time."

Ellie stood up straight, a rabbit-caught-in-the-headlights look in her eyes.

"You're right," Reece grumbled. "Let's go and find them and get this over with. I'm getting bored."

Callum sat frozen as he listened to their voices drift away. "They've gone upstairs," he said, craning his neck to look at the ceiling. Two pairs of heavy footsteps echoed above them. "We have to go, now."

"Did you hear what they said? About last time?"

"Yeah." A memory itched at his brain. "They mentioned a cleaning cupboard. Where did I see … oh, wait, you don't think they had something to do with that article, do you? The one that was shared on the Deddit thread?"

"Yeah," Ellie whispered, still staring at the door as she ran her fingers along the silver chain on her wrist. "I do. I didn't want it to be true, but…" she trailed off.

"Ellie? Why do I get the feeling you haven't told me something?"

She sighed, collecting the bloody tissues from around the room and pushing them through the lid into the bin. Callum noticed a smear of red on the plastic. He really hoped his mum wouldn't be the one to clean up after him if this all went horribly wrong.

"Because I haven't," Ellie said simply.

"Well, tell me now," he said, gritting his teeth against the throbbing in his side.

"OK. But I want you to know I wasn't hiding it or anything, I promise. Her name was Alice. The girl from the article. She was my best friend." A wave of nausea swept over Callum, forcing him to grab the desk chair as he stared at her.

"What do you mean?"

"Exactly what I said. Alice was my best friend and

she died at a Halloween party. I never believed she killed herself and now…" She shook her head slowly, tears streaming down her face. "I think it was them. I think they killed her."

 chat

Outbox (@WitchesBrew_2007)
>Direct message< 27/10/2021 20:59
To: CreepyTeepee
Hey!
I know you don't come on here much, but I want to add you to this cool chat I'm in.
I've met some awesome people who recommended loads of spooooooooky games for the Halloween party!

Inbox (@WitchesBrew_2007)
>Direct message< 27/10/2021 22:35,
From: CreepyTeepee

I got your text.
You've not added me to anything, have you? You know I hate this hell site.

Outbox (@WitchesBrew_2007)
>Direct message< 27/10/2021 22:41
To: CreepyTeepee
Not yet.
Come on! I promise it won't be like last time.
You're a big girl now.

 chat

Yeah, a big girl who still has nightmares about that creepy pasta who cut off his own eyelids and whispered "Go to sleeeeep" when he killed people.

Outbox (@WitchesBrew_2007)

>Direct message< 27/10/2021 22:45

To: CreepyTeepee

OK, yes. I admit that probably wasn't the best thing to show you at a sleepover. But it was, like, five years ago.

Come on. Some of these games are so spooky!

Inbox (@WitchesBrew_2007)

>Direct message< 27/10/2021 22:50

From: CreepyTeepee

Nope.

Outbox (@WitchesBrew_2007)

>Direct message< 27/10/2021 22:52

To: CreepyTeepee

Pleeeeeeease?

L?

Ellieeeeeeee.

Eleanor...

 chat

---

Inbox (@WitchesBrew_2007)

>Direct message< 27/10/2021 22:59

From: CreepyTeepee

Do not full name me, Alice Rose Gooding.
One question: if you add me now, will I be able to see the rest of the chat?

Outbox (@WitchesBrew_2007)

>Direct message< 27/10/2021 23:00

To: CreepyTeepee
Er…
No, actually. I don't think you will. Just everything after you join.

Inbox (@WitchesBrew_2007)

>Direct message< 27/10/2021 23:02

From: CreepyTeepee

No point then, is there?
Just show me at college tomorrow.

Outbox (@WitchesBrew_2007)

>Direct message< 27/10/2021 23:03

To: CreepyTeepee
Oh, fine. They're really cool to chat to, though.

301

Inbox (@WitchesBrew_2007)
>Direct message< 27/10/2021 23:05
From: CreepyTeepee

Al?

Please tell me you haven't told internet randos we're having a party?

Outbox (@WitchesBrew_2007)
>Direct message< 27/10/2021 23:06
To: CreepyTeepee
Of course not.

Inbox (@WitchesBrew_2007)
>Direct message< 27/10/2021 23:07
From: CreepyTeepee

Are you sure? You make bad internet decisions, remember? We've only just stopped doing damage control from when your Insta priv account got hacked...

Outbox (@WitchesBrew_2007)
>Direct message< 27/10/2021 23:09
To: CreepyTeepee
You don't have to remind me.
I wasn't allowed my phone unsupervised for months.

 chat

---

Inbox (@WitchesBrew_2007)
>Direct message< 27/10/2021 23:10
From: CreepyTeepee

OK, good.
Honestly, I don't even know why I still have an account on here.
It's nightmare fuel.

Outbox (@WitchesBrew_2007)
>Direct message< 27/10/2021 23:12
To: CreepyTeepee
Which is exactly why we like it…

Inbox (@WitchesBrew_2007)
>Direct message< 27/10/2021 23:14
From: CreepyTeepee

Yeah, yeah, I know.
In small doses.
In the daytime…

Outbox (@WitchesBrew_2007)
>Direct message< 27/10/2021 23:16
To: CreepyTeepee
Oh, fine.
I'll show you tomorrow.
Night xo

 chat

Night, sweetie xo

TONI

"What was that?"

"What? Stop being so jumpy. I knew I shouldn't have let you smoke," Reece snapped at her as he led the way along the upstairs corridor. He was hyped up, flinging open office doors so far that they bounced off the walls on the other side.

"But I needed to calm down," she whispered, trying not to wince every time a door swung. "All that adrenaline... I needed something to take the edge off."

They passed the final office and emerged into the open space of the upstairs foyer. Streetlights shone through the windows that lined the front wall, and Toni could see that it had started to drizzle outside. A car droned past, just

305

audible through a pair of thin wooden doors that led out on to a small stone balcony.

"How far could they have got?" Reece growled. He peered into the large dark hall. Toni could see the scuffed salt circle on the floor but other than that and the creeping shadows it was empty.

"They must have gone the opposite way. Maybe we keep missing them. Or" – a realization struck her – "they've left. Gone to the police."

"No, I don't think so. They believed that whole Midnight Man thing too much to go outside." Reece rubbed a hand across his chin. "I mean, look at the salt they left behind in the staffroom. No, they're still in here somewhere, scurrying around like little rats."

"Maybe." Toni's skin prickled as she watched him head towards the corridor where the girl's body was. She paused. What if they *had* escaped?

What if they told someone?

Surely now was the time for damage control. Maybe Toni should look out for herself for a change. The girl in the art room, Mei. That had all been Reece's doing; Toni had been with Hugo and the others when Reece had killed her. Then he'd murdered Hugo too. Toni had nothing to do with anyone actually getting slaughtered, did she? She forced down the heat that rose from her stomach as she thought of the first scene. Overkill. She'd read that somewhere once and hadn't understood what it meant until she'd seen the mess he'd made.

He was out of control.

"Come out, come out, wherever you are." Reece's monotone sing-song floated along the corridor. "Or I'll huff … and I'll puff…"

Toni weighed up her choices. The stairs were right there. She could be down and out of the hut in less than a minute. She could be the one who went to the police – after all, all she'd really done tonight was stab that Callum kid, and last time she'd only held the girl still. Reece had been the one who'd dragged the blade across her wrists. She could still make something up; it wasn't too late. She could say that Reece had coerced her. Threatened her or something. Even better, she could say she meant to stab *Reece*, and Callum just got in the way. She was actually trying to stop the crazed killer…

A dark shadow filled the entrance to the hall.

"Hello?" She said it without thinking. As if they would answer her. Reece was down the corridor; she could hear his footsteps echoing down there. So, who was it? Was it possible that he'd missed them when they looked in the hall? He was high as a kite, after all. He must not have looked properly. "Callum?" She tried. "Ellie? I'm … I'm sorry." She took a step closer, making her voice small. "I'm scared too."

The shadow melted into the dark room.

"Toni," it breathed.

She turned and looked at the stairs, her skin prickling. She was paranoid and they were playing with her; they had to be.

"Toniiiiiii." The sound slithered out through the doorway, as though it had a mind of its own. "Toniiiiiiiiiii."

"Stop it!" She took a step towards the doorway, pausing to take a breath. The darkness in there was slick now, long fingers of inky blackness reaching out to her. She rubbed her eyes. Jesus, whatever she had smoked was strong. "I'm sorry, really." She tried to inject a note of regret into her voice as she inched into the large room.

A breeze ran over her, gently lifting tendrils of her hair. Almost like someone was breathing right in her face. She swallowed. "I didn't mean to hurt you, Callum. I was trying to stab Reece, to stop him." Another breath from the far corner, almost a wheeze this time. "I want to help you get out of here."

"Liar," a voice hissed from behind her.

Toni whipped around. "Ellie, is that you? I'm telling the truth, I swear! We need to get out of here. Reece – he's lost it. Maybe the game got to him or something." She squinted towards where the sound had come from but could see nothing except darkness.

For the first time she wished she'd kept hold of a candle.

"Liar," the voice repeated. It came from the corner again, where she thought she'd heard Callum whimper.

"I promise." She tried a sob, but it sounded phoney even to her own ears. She had to do a better job if she wanted to get out of this mess. Her eyes finally adjusted, and the outline of a crouched figure began to come into view. "Oh, Callum, I'm so sorry," she tried, her eyes tracing the shape of the boy in the corner, his arms wrapped around tucked-in knees. "Let me help you."

She held her breath as the figure began to unfold. He didn't seem to be badly injured; maybe she hadn't really hurt him before. That would help her story. She held a hand out as the dark mass reached its full height. Wait. This wasn't right.

It kept unfolding.

"No," she breathed. The figure was dispersing before her eyes into sinuous wisps and shadows. It seemed to melt into the air, losing any sense of shape, before rushing back together to form the shadow of a man.

"Where is your candle?" The deep, creaking voice was mocking her, almost teasing, but there was a guillotine sharpness to it. "Have you broken the rules?"

"Stop it!" Toni shouted. She shut her eyes, wishing that she hadn't agreed to any of this, especially the weed. She took a deep breath. She needed to clear her head.

A cool hand caressed her throat.

Toni's eyes popped open and the scream she had felt rising died in her throat. The face before her stretched into an impossible smile, the edges of its mouth carving into the stretched shadow flesh. "Rule breakers must be punished," it rasped as Toni found her voice.

"Reece!" she screamed. The shadow man broke apart and Toni whirled on her heel and headed back to the corridor. She looked straight ahead, desperate to ignore the malevolent shadow forming by the door. "Reece!" Her voice cracked, the last part of his name swallowed by her distress. She closed her eyes and burst through the open doorway, the toe of her boot catching on a piece of carpet that had lifted at the threshold.

"You must be punished." The shadow settled around her like a cloak as she hit the floor and she realized she was no longer hearing the words aloud. *They were inside her head.* Toni sobbed and tried to push herself off the floor with the palms of her hands. She winced at the pain, her knees and the heels of her hands skinned raw from the rough carpet, but she gritted her teeth and tried to force her way through the fog that pinned her there. *You have done wrong.* The voice was grating now, so deep in her brain that Toni wasn't sure if she was possessed or if she'd just finally lost it. *You broke the rules. You injured another. You must pay.*

"How?" Toni screamed, lumbering to her feet. A cold breeze stung the cuts on her knees, and she glanced up towards the windows where the light filtered in. How did she not notice the balcony doors were open before?

With your life.

"Reece," Toni sobbed. It was real this time, the sob. The fear. She was in trouble. "Reece, help me."

Run, little girl.

It was right. The shadow, the voice – whatever it was. She had to get out of here. She wiped her eyes and tried to run towards the staircase, but her knees turned to jelly and she hit the banister instead. Her stomach slammed into the thick wooden balustrade and the air rushed out of her lungs, forcing her to crumple on the spot. She grasped at the wrought-iron railings and looked down into the lower part of the school. The way out was down there, tantalizingly close. If she could just reach it…

What are you frightened of? The thought pierced her consciousness as Toni pushed up to her feet once more.

"As if I'd tell you," she wheezed to the shadows. They were closing in again and every time Toni looked away that too-wide smile danced in the edges of her vision. She forced her legs forward until she reached the top of the landing. She was aiming to run down the stairs and straight out the front door. She didn't care if it was alarmed or not. As she pulled herself along the railing, the balcony doors slammed against one another, opening wide again as she realized it was lashing down with rain now, the wind whipping in.

You don't have to tell me. It's all in here…

"Stop!" Toni screamed as a white-hot pain pushed deep into her head, probing fingers of agony that blinded her immediately. She scrunched her eyes to stop the torture and reached out her hands as the weight of the shadow settled over her again. Her fingers closed around the edge of the balcony door as she felt her way along, the windowpane slick beneath her grasp. "Help," she wheezed, pushing herself forwards so her voice might be heard outside. "Please, help me."

Don't fall.

She twisted around, her back to the balcony, and forced her eyelids apart as she realized the shooting pain had gone. The foyer in front of her was empty. Even the wind had died down. The throbbing in her head subsided and she could hear someone – probably Reece – clattering around downstairs, turning over furniture in an effort to find his prey. She took a deep, shaking breath and a laugh bubbled up from her stomach. She really was losing it. She wasn't cut out for this much drama, never mind drugs. She wanted to get home, get this stupid costume off and go to bed. She eyed the stairs once more, unaware of the tendrils gathering around her ankles. She was going to get the hell out of here and put this whole mess behind her.

It's too late.

The blow to Toni's stomach took her breath away. She doubled over, stumbling backwards until she was outside on the small gallery that stuck out over the main entrance of the school. She grasped for something, anything, to hold on to, but the stone railing was too low, barely thigh-height, and slick with rain. She landed on it heavily, wondering if it would take her weight as she scrabbled at the stone with her hands. Toni felt several months of moss and grime come away from the stone beneath her fingers and could do nothing but watch as they started to slip. A dark figure started to form in front of her and a powerful blow to her chest sent her into the air.

Wrongdoers must be punished.

Toni filled her lungs with shadows and screamed all the way down.

Al 17:42
How's the costume coming along?
Any luck with getting a cat flap?

L 17:45
Yep, I ordered one on eBay. I'm hoping it comes in time (and that I fit into it).
It's harder to get a giant cat-flap than you'd think.

Al 17:45
Well, that's not a sentence I ever thought I'd read.
Can we make one if it doesn't come in time?

L 17:46
Good idea!
Why didn't I think of that?
I'll go down and hoard some cardboard later.
Al?

Al 17:46
Yeah?

L 17:46

Do you think those games are real?

Al 17:47

What do you mean?

L 17:48

You know, those games you showed me before.
Do you think anything really happens if you
play them?

Al 17:49

I dunno. I'd like to think so, but … no. I can't
see how they could be.
They're just games to freak people out.

L 17:49

I guess.
So, you don't think it's dangerous to play them?

Al 17:50

Maybe for someone who's not mentally healthy,
I guess.
Or if you're super paranoid.

L 17:51

Yeah.
I mean, I kind of get why someone would play
the ones where you get something at the end.
They'd be worth the risk.

Al 17:52
Do you think so?

L 17:52

Yeah, if you wanted something bad enough.

Al 17:53
Then, yeah. I guess it would be worth it.

L 17:54

The one you've picked doesn't have any of that,
though, does it?
Like, no rewards if you play properly.

Al 17:55
No.
But I'm hoping that I might get something out
of it, anyway.

REECE

Reece had his back to the window when a loud thud shook the ground outside. He snarled in rage.

Someone had got out.

He turned to look outside, expecting to see the front door wide open, or those idiots trying to escape. He flexed his shoulders, twisting his neck from side-to-side to loosen up. He was in good shape; he could outrun either of them, especially if they were injured or ill.

But there was no one out there.

"What the hell?" he mumbled, leaning so close to the pane that his breath fogged up the glass. It was raining heavily out there, and between the streetlights and the sloughing water, Reece could just make out a black-clad

317

figure lying outside on the steps that led to the entrance. "Toni?"

He craned his neck to look up. From here he could just about see that the balcony doors were swinging open. The small curve of stone jutted out over the wide steps. He stared back at Toni's broken body, her limbs bent at impossible angles. Her head was twisted, staring accusingly at him from the bottom step. She looked like a marionette that had had its strings cut. He looked at the balcony again and realized that she must have fallen.

Or maybe she'd been pushed.

"You're dead!" The roar tore out of him as he grabbed hold of a table, flipping it towards the wall, small blue plastic chairs flying through the air. "You hear me? I'm coming for you!"

Reece burst into the corridor, chest heaving, and looked both ways. It was still, no signs of life anywhere.

They couldn't be far, though.

"There's no point in hiding," he shouted as he stormed towards the foyer. He climbed the stairs two at a time, pausing at the open balcony doors. "I saw what you did to Toni. I was going to kill you both before, but *now* I'll make sure it's painful."

Nothing. He pushed the balcony doors closed and gave himself a second to listen without the wind interfering.

There.

There was a shuffling sound in the hall, barely audible

but he had heard it. He slid a hand into his pocket and pulled out the flick knife. It was tacky in his fingers.

"Run," he crooned as he crossed the threshold into the large room. It appeared empty, but he gave it a second, letting his eyes adjust to the dark corners. Stupid candle would have come in useful now.

Nothing.

"Come out," he whispered, moving back into the hall. Maybe he should try a different tactic, be quiet. Bide his time.

He began to mentally retrace his steps. He'd looked everywhere. No – not everywhere. One of the doors had been locked. There was only one place he hadn't checked.

The cleaning cupboard.

"I knew it," he hissed. They must have found another key; he should have realized there would be spares. If he hadn't listened to Toni, they wouldn't be in this mess. The silly cow would probably still be alive. His blood boiled at the thought. What a waste. Nobody would *ever* understand him like she had.

Someone was going to pay.

Reece turned into the corridor towards the staircase they had used after they abandoned the locked room. He climbed down slowly this time, as quiet as a church-mouse, and eased open the door into the main corridor.

The painted door was directly in front of him,

wide-open and taunting. Reece felt a roar of anger well up inside him as he looked into what was clearly a medical room. It was empty now, but there was a used roll of duct tape, an open bottle of Calpol and a scattering of torn paper packets on a worn desk in the corner. Not just that – there was another door.

And it was open.

His brain whirred. If they got away he was screwed. They'd actually seen him kill the posh kid, and it would be two against one if they talked. He could blame the other kill on Toni, it wasn't like she'd mind now. He was almost out of the playground door when he looked back to the table and paused.

Candles.

Two small, artificial candles sat on top of the desk. He picked one up and flicked the switch, but nothing happened. Same with the other one. Now, why would there be broken candles in a medical room?

Reece turned back the way he'd come and stopped at the door to the staffroom. There. The bloody salt circle. His mouth dropped as he realized that they really were still playing the game.

That was a clever move, though. They'd left the door open in the hope that he would go outside looking for them and they could wait in the building until 3:33. He checked his watch – almost three twenty. They clearly had a plan. He couldn't believe they really bought into this kiddy rubbish – he bet they'd taken the working candles with them and left the duds behind. Ellie might have even got hold of some insulin in that room, God knows what they kept in schools these days.

Thirteen minutes to go until they made a break for it. He wandered back to the foyer, swinging the knife loosely between his fingers as he walked to the main door, a huge wooden thing. As he thought about Toni's body splayed out on the other side of it, he realized she was his way out. He'd deal with the other two as soon as he found them and then write a note. Poor, unstable Toni had killed them all in a drug-induced psychosis and when she came around, she couldn't bear the guilt – so she had thrown herself off the balcony.

No one even needed to know he had been there.

He wondered about his fingerprints for a second but dismissed the thought – there must be hundreds of sets of prints around the building, and he didn't have a criminal record so they'd probably be disregarded. He just needed something to write with and to finish what he had started.

That was it. He'd checked everywhere but the place they had started.

The hut.

It made total sense. It was easy to get out, the doors weren't alarmed, but it was still technically a part of the building. They wouldn't break the going outside rule, but he bet they were in there, ready to run when the clock hit 3:33.

Well, not any more.

He started heading towards the door that would lead him to the makeshift corridor. Shadows curled around the ceiling, but he knew that was down to a lack of light. Nothing else.

"Reece?"

He turned back to the foyer. "Toni? Is that you?"

"Reece! It's me." A long, slow wail crept in through the cracks around the front door. "Help, I'm hurt…" The wail continued, low and agonizing. Reece reached a hand towards it. "Come out and help me."

He dropped his hand.

"What did you say?"

"Come outside. I need you." The wail turned to thick, guttural sobs and Reece felt the hairs on his arms stand up. If Toni was hurt, wouldn't she be asking to come in, instead? A cold breeze wrapped around his arms as he heard her again.

"Reece," she hissed.

This time the voice was behind him.

He turned quickly, knife raised, but it sliced harmlessly through the air. It was them; it had to be. They were messing with him, trying to freak him out. Well, screw them. He'd go on the run to Spain or something; he could just leave. They couldn't arrest someone who wasn't around, and he'd deleted all his accounts online, plus he ran everything through a VPN. They'd have a hard time tracing him at all.

He ran back to the door that led to the hut, the voice hissing at him all the way down the corridor.

Al 16:42
Did the cat flap come?
And how are you feeling?

L 16:43
Yeah, it did!
Mum was a bit confused, but even she
admitted it was a fun costume.
Also, cramps = sad face.

Al 16:44
Take some painkillers! Dr Alice says so.
Oh, by the way, your mum knows you're staying
at mine tomorrow, right?

L 16:44
I have. Thanks, doc.
And yeah, she does, but only cos she rang your
mum to check.

Al 16:45
Well, we're not lying about the sleepover bit,
are we?
Just where the party is.
And what we're doing there.

L 16:46

This is all very true.

Do you think we're gonna get bollocked for staying out so late?

I mean, it'll be 4 a.m. at least if we play that game.

AI 16:47

Probably, but have you heard that saying?

"Better to apologize after than to ask permission before."

Or something like that.

L 16:50

Ha, no.

You totally made that up.

But I like it.

AI 16:52

I thought you would.

Send me a cat flap pic.

AI 17:23

Hello?

AI 18:00

El? You OK?

Text me when you're back online x

L 22:53

OMG I'm so sorry.
I totally fell asleep with the phone on my face.
I'm shattered.

Al 22:55
Hey! Don't worry!
Is it your period? Are the cramps still bad?

L 22:56

I'm literally dying.
My period hasn't even bothered to make an appearance yet.
It's probably waiting to bloat me out tomorrow night.
Back in bed with a hot water bottle. The joy.

Al 22:57
I'm sorry, honey, that sucks.
Hopefully they'll be gone by tomorrow!

L 22:59

They'd better be!
My outfit does not allow for bloating.

A 23:01
Of course it doesn't…
Go and get some sleep. I'll FaceTime you tomorrow.

L 23:02
OK.
Night, honey.

Saturday 30th October 2021

L 04:32
Al?
Sorry, I know it's late.
I'm in hospital. Pains are bad and I can't stop spewing.
Mum worried.
Text me when you're up.

L 05:53
Al?
I'm going into surgery – burst appendix.
I can't come to the party.

L 06:01
Love you xo

ELLIE

Ellie squeezed Callum's hand, unsure whether she was comforting him or hanging on for dear life. Probably both. Shock was starting to take over now, and Ellie felt completely adrift. For the first time in for ever she had no idea what her blood sugar was or if she was minutes away from a hyper or even worse, a hypo.

"The game's almost over." Callum squeezed back weakly. "We'll be out of here in no time."

"Yeah."

"I … I still can't believe what we saw. Can you?"

"No. I know we kind of thought that the game was real but … to see Toni like that…" Ellie shuddered, Toni screaming and crying as she fell through the window replaying on a loop in her brain.

"I know. And the shadows…"

"Don't." They were crammed into one of the little music rooms now. After they'd stumbled upon Toni fighting – whatever that was – in the upstairs foyer, Callum had dragged her back into the hall, and through a hidden door that led back down to the old cells. They'd listened as Reece tore up and down the hallways, but it had fallen mysteriously quiet a few minutes ago. After seeing Toni fall from the window, neither of them were quite willing to leave yet. Ellie looked down at their sad plastic candles. "Well, either we found the all-time greatest hack with these things or he's just not after us."

"Reece? Or the Midnight Man?"

"Good point." She let go of him and ran her hand through her hair, fingers catching where it had matted together. She didn't want to think about what had turned it into such a knotted mess. "Hear me out. What if the game *is* real—"

"Which it is," Callum interrupted, "we just saw—"

"I know, I know. But that's what I mean. If the game is real, why target Toni? I broke a rule – I was unconscious – and we didn't have candles for ages."

Callum started counting reasons on his fingers. "Well, two people were already … dead … so they wouldn't be targeted. We were in a salt circle when you were breaking the rules, but Toni wasn't. And we had candles, even though they're fake, but she didn't. She left herself wide open."

"You're right. Reece won't be following the rules any more either, I guarantee it. He thinks this is *his* game; we know that from reading his note. But he's the wrongdoer – he's the kind of person the Midnight Man would want to punish."

"Just like Toni," Callum breathed.

"But he's worse. Yeah, she stabbed me, but he *murdered* Mei and Hugo."

"And Alice."

Callum shuffled slightly. "Ellie, can I ask you a personal question?"

"Why not? I think we're firm friends now." The shadow of a smile quirked her lips.

"Why are you here? After Alice died playing the game? I know you didn't know she'd been killed, but if it was my best friend I don't think I'd even utter the name of the game, let alone play it."

"Until tonight I didn't know if I actually would play. I guess joining the Deddit thread was morbid curiosity. Al loved that stupid website, so it was almost a way to keep her alive." Ellie reached back into her bra, extracting a slip of bloodstained paper. "I didn't really know what I was here for until I wrote this." She held it out to him.

"I don't have to read that. It was your secret."

"I'll trade you."

Callum hesitated and Ellie wondered what he wasn't telling her.

"OK." He took the paper from her fingers and held it as close to his eyes as he could manage. "Well, looks like your secret is safe. There's not enough light in here to read it."

"Oh." Ellie licked her lips nervously. She needed someone to know why she was here, just in case. "It says something like *'I wanted to feel how she felt before she died.'*"

"Oh, Ellie," Callum whispered.

"I felt so guilty and now I know what they did to her … how am I supposed to live with that?"

"I'm so sorry you found out that way." Callum looked at her with genuine pity, but she just felt hollow inside. The scene of Alice trapped with Reece and Toni was tattooed into her thoughts. "It's not your fault you weren't with her."

"I know that, but I don't think I'll ever stop thinking it was. You know she tried to call me that night? But I didn't answer."

"You were in the hospital! You can't blame yourself for that."

"I know." Ellie brushed away a tear in defiance, sniffling back the rest. "Your turn. What did you write?"

Callum slid two pieces of paper over to her. "Keep that safe with yours. We need to burn them when this game is over, right?"

"OK." Ellie put the papers back into her bra. "So, what

does it say? Why are you here?"

"I suppose you'd call it a test of faith."

"What do you mean?"

He took a deep breath. "I've been doing a lot of soul-searching recently."

"In what way?"

"Religion. I wasn't really brought up in a religion, but my dad was – maybe still is, who knows? – a Muslim. I remember watching him pray when I was little. He left when I was a kid, and I haven't heard from him since so that was that. Mum was broken, but she'd never show it. She never remarried or anything. Last year I made some friends at football who are Muslim and started getting curious about my dad again. I started to read up about it and suddenly I felt … I dunno, connected to a part of my heritage or something. I couldn't tell Mum, though. I think she'd be gutted that I wanted to be like him. So I've kept it a secret."

"And tonight was for what? To see if gods and demons actually exist?"

"I guess so. If this was all for real and I survived, then maybe god is real too?"

"Then you could tell your mum about it with a little less guilt?" Ellie asked.

"Yeah." He wiped a tear from the corner of his eye. "Bit extreme."

"I think we've bonded over extreme." Ellie reached for

his hand again, and this time he took it without hesitation, sliding his fingers between hers. "Your mum will love you no matter what you believe in. You should tell her."

"I will." He eyed the door. "If we ever get out of here."

"Oh, we're getting out of here. Someone has to pay for their wrongdoings."

Callum narrowed his eyebrows. "What do you mean?"

"I mean Reece. He killed my best friend and got away with it. He killed Mei, who had her whole life ahead of her. She was fourteen for God's sake! And Hugo, who was just trying to do better. Maybe he wasn't the best person, but he didn't deserve to be slaughtered like that. If Reece thinks he's going to do it again, to us or anyone else, he's got another thing coming."

"Go on."

"I have a plan. We can let him get what's coming to him. Go to the police. Get justice for Al and the others. You in?"

Callum nodded. "Hell, yes, I'm in. Just tell me what to do."

★★★

"You're clear on the plan?" Ellie asked as she stood in front of the door that led to the hut. She looked down the long prefab corridor. Callum followed her slowly.

"Yeah. Are you sure he's down there?"

"He must be. He'll expect us to try and leave that way,

it's the only unlocked door in the place."

"Apart from the medical room. But you're right, I don't think he bought that trick."

"No. So this is it." Ellie looked at her watch. Three thirty. They had three minutes.

"Ellie? Do you mind if I pray for us first?"

"Not at all."

Callum held his free hand out, palm slightly open. Ellie caught hold of it as he closed his eyes, realizing too late that she had mistaken the gesture, but he didn't shake her off. If anything she hoped it would make the prayer stronger. He repeated the dua he had recited in the medical room and when he opened his eyes, Ellie leaned over and gave him a peck on the cheek.

"Thank you." He looked at her with big brown eyes.

God, she hoped they would both get out of this.

"Let's go," he said. He led the way into the corridor and she followed, trying to keep her steps quiet, but the floor bounced and swayed beneath them. She hung back slightly, allowing Callum to rush through the door like they had planned.

"About time you two showed up," Reece snarled.

He stood in the centre of the unused classroom. He looked dishevelled, dark stains all over his tracksuit bottoms and brown hair sticking out from every angle. His eyes were wild as Callum charged towards him, swinging the rounders bat they'd salvaged from the staffroom. Ellie took her cue and darted past them both, towards the door that led on to the playground. She heard a sickening thump and a body hit the floor. She continued, hoping it was Reece's head that had made the crunching sound and darted out of the door, pressing her back up to the side of the little entrance porch. Not technically outside, but close enough.

"Ell-ieeee." No! Reece's voice floated out on to the playground and Ellie felt sick in the pit of her stomach.

She inched to the small, grimy window and strained her eyes to see in through the scratched plexiglass. Callum lay face down on the rough carpet, a shadow blooming around his head. Ellie clapped a hand to her mouth.

The alarm on Callum's digital watch started beeping.

"Game over, princess." Reece chuckled, walking slowly to the door. Ellie glanced out into the playground and adjusted her position slightly. There – perfect. "That's it, you stay right there," he crooned as he spotted her. "Maybe we can have some fun before I finish you."

Ellie stopped breathing as Reece walked past her. He clattered down the porch steps and into the playground. That was it … he just needed to take one more step…

"Hey, what is this?" He paused in front of the mirror, his short, squat reflection staring back at him.

"Didn't you read the rules, Reece?" Ellie snarled from the doorway. Her reflection in the playground mirror had worked – he was outside, and she wasn't. He turned to face her, fury at being tricked twisting his features. "*Rule number three: don't go outside.*"

"What?" Reece lunged at her, but his feet stayed glued to the asphalt. Ellie was frozen as she watched what looked like tendrils of smoke curl around Reece's arms and legs. "What the hell is this?"

"You broke the rules," she said.

"But it's not real," he shouted, squirming, the coils of black creeping up to his midsection. Ellie heard a groan behind her and turned to see Callum pushing up to his knees.

"You're the wrongdoer," Ellie screamed at Reece, her voice whipping away on the wind. "You killed the person I loved most in this world and then you kept on going. You deserve to be ripped apart."

"Help me!" Reece's eyes were bulging now, wraithlike hands wrapped around his waist. "It can't be real … even if it is, your watch went off! The game's over!"

"False alarm," Callum rasped, joining Ellie on the porch. "There's still one minute left."

"No." Reece tried to get the word out, but a long tendril of smoke forced its way into his mouth, over his teeth and tongue until he was choking. Ellie and Callum watched in awe as he fought the shadows before going completely still.

"Cover your eyes," Callum ordered.

Ellie dropped to the floor and buried her head in her hands as a loud, wet ripping sound filled the air. She stayed there for a second, trying to ignore the wet flecks that splashed on her arms.

The alarm on Callum's watch started to beep again.

"Three thirty-three," he croaked. "Game over."

She stood up next to Callum and pulled the scraps from her pocket, the secrets she had collected. He thrust another pile of paper into Ellie's hands, some still punctured with brass drawing pins. Their names. He struck a match, and she began to feed them into the flame one by one.

Mei.

Hugo.

Callum.

Ellie.

"Is that it?" she asked. "Shouldn't we do theirs, too? Free them?"

"They don't deserve it," Callum said.

Ellie hesitated before nodding. "Agreed." She set the last two pieces of paper alight together, allowing the flames to lick the secrets right down to her fingers before she dropped them on to the ground.

"Game over."

"Game over," she echoed. "Are you OK?" Ellie put both hands on his shoulders, her forgotten candle hitting the ground with a tap.

"Yeah, it's just a gash." His eyebrow was split open and already swelling into a ledge over his eye. "It just needs some pressure on it. He nearly knocked me out, though."

"Is … is he dead?" She refused to turn her head. "I can't look."

"I'd be amazed if he wasn't." Callum retched. Now she definitely wasn't going to look. "Let's get the hell out of here."

Ellie ducked under Callum's arm and helped him down the steps, eyes firmly on the ground. The smell of death was enough; she didn't need to see Reece's body.

Then she spotted Toni.

"Go to my car." She reached into her top and handed Callum a small set of keys. "It's the blue Fiesta, down there. I'll just be a sec."

"Seriously, what else have you got in there?" Ellie smirked and he blushed. "I didn't mean … oh, just hurry up."

She watched him limp over to the gate as she approached Toni's body. A roll of paper lay on the steps next to her and Ellie bent to pick it up, unrolling it. It was the other girl's secret.

I want to keep Reece happy.

"Pathetic," Ellie spat. She looked down at what she had really come for, her gaze settling on the thin, silver chain that glinted on the other girl's snapped neck. Ellie reached down, tugging it off with a little more force than she would have liked. The ends came apart and she stood up straight, holding it over her wrist, the jagged half of a heart finally finding its mate again.

"I think you'll find that's mine." She stared down at the dead girl. "Bitch."

Saturday 30th October 2021

Al 08:14
ELLIE!
Shit.
Ringing you.

Missed voice call from Al

Al 08:16
Text me when you can!

L 10:43
Out.
Spewy.
Sleep.

Al 10:43
OH, THANK GOD.

L 10:57
Spk sn

Al 10:58
Ssh, just sleep, honey.

Al 14:00
How's the patient?

L 14:52

Yo.
Off my teats on morphine.

Al 14:53

What the hell happened?

L 14:59

Period cramps were not period cramps.
They took out my appendix.
Sorry so slow.
Can't see straight.

Al 15:00

I'm so sorry, El!
How long are you in for?

L 15:06

Dunno.
Few days?

Al 15:07

I'll come and visit later!

L 15:10

Don't you dare!
You have your party.

Al 15:10
Not without you!
I wanted you to be there!
It won't be the same.

L 15:16
Al, I am useless right now.
Do NOT miss the party of the century for me.
Promise?

Al 15:17
But I feel awful!

L 15:19
Well, don't.
I will not allow it.

Al 15:20
Can I come see you tomorrow?

L 15:22
With a stinking hangover and looking worse
than I do?
'Course you can.

Al 15:24
Aw, El! I'm gutted!

L 15:26
I know, me too.
Just glad not to be in pain.

Al 15:27
I'm so glad you're OK.

L 15:30
Me too.
Send me party pics!
Think I need more sleep.

Al 15:33
OK you rest.
See you tomorrow x

Sunday 31st October 2021

Al 03:27
Ellie?
I need you, help me.

Missed voice call from Al

Al 03:29
El?
I'm worried I'll never see you again.
Ellie – I love you. Like, more than a friend love
you.
I'm sorry I never told you before.

Al 03:33
I love y

CALLUM

Callum emerged from the shadows. He slunk past the playground gates, slow, almost melting into the night. His progress was deliberate, but painful. One leg dragging, a harsh, hollow wheezing emanating from his chest.

He did not look back.

Slowly, like blood trickling from a puncture wound, Callum stopped. Rested. A jangle of keys cleared the air, somehow chasing away the encroaching darkness, the horror of the night.

He pulled open the car door and climbed inside.

He did not look back.

It was cold in the car, and his numb fingers fumbled as if on automatic, sliding the keys into the ignition and twisting until the engine reluctantly roared to life. He locked the doors, a comforting click that promised safety, then turned the heater on. Callum twisted the dial all the way around, relishing the white noise in his ears, and burrowed down, waiting for the air to lose its chill.

He did not look back. Instead, he pulled down the sun visor. There was no sun, of course, at almost 3:40 a.m., but there was a picture, a photograph stashed up there. In it there were two figures, though he knew that one of them was very definitely dead.

Callum's skin shrank on his bones as nails tapped on the window. He forced his eyes open, grateful to see it was only Ellie.

"I put the heater on," he explained as she climbed into the driver's seat. "I'm cold."

"You need a doctor. You've lost a lot of blood."

"Yeah."

They sat in silence for a second as Ellie held her own hands out, soaking in the warm air. She glanced up at the visor, her mouth twisting in a sad smile.

"Was that her?" Callum asked gently. "Alice?"

"Yeah." She pulled the photo down. "She was my favourite person."

"She looks nice."

"She was the best." A tear fell down Ellie's cheek. "You know she text me before she died? Told me she loved me."

"Like, romantic loved you?" Callum asked and Ellie nodded slightly. "Did you like her that way?"

She hesitated. "I don't know. I never … had time to think about it. I loved her with every fibre of my being, I'd just never thought of anyone like *that*, you know? Let alone Al."

Callum nodded. "Me either. Love is scary. Do you think you might have, though? If she was still here?"

"That's what kills me. I'll never know now, will I?" She sighed, running a hand over the picture. "This was only last summer. We'd just got our exam results." It showed them in all their mis-matched glory – Alice: pale, dark hair and make-up, head to toe black, even in August. Ellie's blonde hair up in a messy bun, flashing a belly-ring in shorts and a crop top. But their smiles were wide and matching and their faces were pressed together in the selfie. "I remember that night so well; we had so much fun."

"I'm sorry." Callum shifted in his seat.

"No, I'm sorry, you're in pain. Come on – hospital."

"What about all that?" He gestured back to the school.

"I really don't know." Ellie shifted gears and looked out of her window before pulling the car out on to the road. "We'll worry about that when we have to."

They turned out on to the main road.

They didn't look back.

Monday 4th July 2022

MASSACRE AT ST. MARTIN'S
Local retiree finds mutilated bodies at local primary school.

By Jessica Johnson

The bodies of four mutilated teenagers were discovered in the early hours of Sunday morning at a local primary school.

The children, believed to have been aged between 14 and 18, have been identified and their families informed.

The gruesome discovery at St. Martin's Roman Catholic Primary School in Prestbury was made by Errol Gardener, 72, who lives close to the school. The retiree found two of the bodies in the playground, and police then discovered another two bodies inside the school building.

He said: "I was walking my dog when I saw them. They were in a right mess. I couldn't really look, it was that bad, so I just called the police straight away. Apparently, there were two more inside the school. I just can't believe it. No one can."

The school will be closed for the rest of term while the police conduct their investigations.

Neighbours say that at least one of the bodies inside the

school was discovered surrounded by a circle of salt, but police have yet to confirm the rumours.

The news comes after the death of Alice Gooding in October – who was also found in a "ritualistic" crime scene. Police have declined to comment on a possible connection.

More to follow.

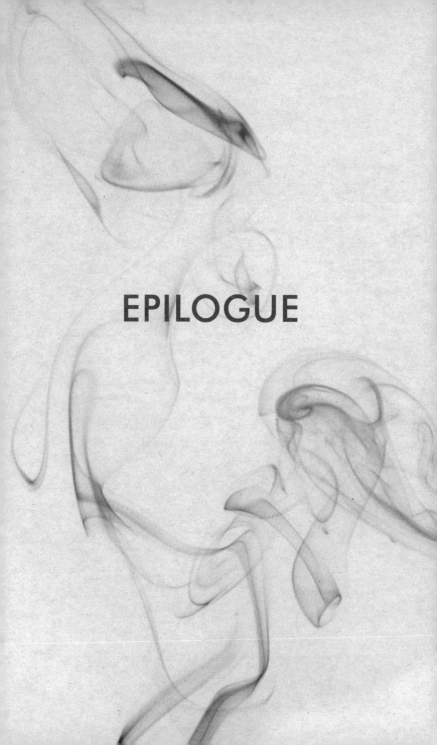

EPILOGUE

ELLIE

"Thank you for coming with me."

Ellie and Callum climbed back into her car. It was dark already, of course, October bleeding into November before their very eyes. Callum buckled his seat belt and twisted to face her.

"Of course. That's what boyfriends are for, right?"

"Among other things," she teased, leaning forward to kiss him. He kissed her back gently before breaking away and tucking a strand of hair behind her ear. She stared back at him, wondering how she'd got so lucky. Callum had said love was scary, but with him? It really wasn't.

"Seriously, how are you feeling?" he asked. "It's been a whole year since you lost her."

"I'm OK, I think." Ellie looked down at the memorial booklet in her lap. Alice's beaming face stared back at her. "She would have liked you, you know."

"I would have liked her," he replied. Ellie leaned back as he loosely threaded his fingers through hers. "I'm so glad her parents have some closure now. It must be so hard for them."

"Yeah." Ellie chewed on her lip. "Cal? You know how we sometimes talk about that night? Do you ever wonder why it didn't work the first time? When Al played with them, I mean. Why didn't the Midnight Man punish them then?"

"I don't know, but I could take a guess. I think they used fake names."

"You do?"

"Yeah." He paused as he rubbed the back of her hand with his thumb in gentle, calming circles. "Remember when Reece introduced himself to you, right before the game even began? I think he messed up. They should have used fake names, but he dropped them in it. I think if they used fake names with Alice, the game probably didn't work as it should have. Names hold a certain kind of power."

"Yeah. Maybe." She rested her head back. "Do you ever wish you could change it all?"

"Of course I do. Well, not all of it." He touched a hand to her chin and gently moved her head so she was facing him again. "I wouldn't change this, you know that, right?

I love you, El."

"I love you too. I really do."

"But?"

"But what if we could bring them back?"

"Wait – El, you can't be serious." Ellie felt Callum's eyes burn into her as she unfolded the sun visor. The photo of her and Alice was still there, just like the chain she wore around her wrist. Al's chain was there too, looped around the little strap that kept the photo in place.

"I found these in the glove compartment. She used to sit in here all the time, even though she hadn't passed her test yet. I'm surprised I didn't find all sorts." Ellie pulled the photo down and revealed a wad of revision cards that she had tucked behind it. They were all written in Alice's precise cursive, beautifully set out and colour coded. She shuffled through them, passing them to Callum so he could read the titles. *The Three Kings Game. One Man Hide and Seek. The Midnight Game. The Eleven Mile Game.*

Ellie stopped at that one.

"You think if The Midnight Game was real, these others are too?"

"I dunno." Callum laughed nervously, his hand unconsciously reaching to his side as it always did now. "Even if they are, I reckon I've had enough for one lifetime. You agree, right?"

"Yeah. Of course." She took the cards from him and replaced them in the visor, putting the photo back in front.

All apart from one.

The Eleven Mile Game.

"What if after you played you got a wish." She turned and looked him in the eye. "What if you could wish that all the bad things that night never happened?"

"But then I wouldn't have you," he said in a small voice.

"You would! We could wish for Mei and Hugo to have survived. I could wish for Al to come back."

Callum was quiet for a second, staring out of the window. He looked back and kissed her gently. "Do you really love me?"

"I really love you," Ellie replied, pressing her lips to his forehead as he leaned into her.

He pulled away and sat up straight. "Then ask me."

Ellie looked him in the eye and forced a wry smile.

"Do you want to play a game?"

ACKNOWLEDGEMENTS

Well, writing a book never gets easier, does it? I really worried I'd been too ambitious with this one and keeping all the threads together really mashed my head, so if you've got this far I hope you've enjoyed reading through the different timelines and formats. It's so different from what I've done before, but I hope it was as fun to read as it was to write. It helps that the designers have done an amazing job as always – the most horrid of stories on the prettiest of pages!

To the thank yous: millions of them must go to the amazing team who turn my bonkers words into beautiful books. My agents, Stephanie Thwaites, Isobel Gahan and Annabel White – more wine, gossip and pizza soon, please! My editor Yasmin Morrissey for being on call for everything from book stuff to restaurant recommendations. You just get everything I do – my fellow weirdo! Thank you to Sarah Dutton for such a conscientious copyedit and Arub Ahmed for proofreading and catching everything that I missed. The errors are definitely mine. Thanks to Lauren Fortune and Sophie Cashell for being such champions of my work and Harriet Dunlea for being excellent at everything – you are a superstar and I'd quite like you to organize the rest of my life, please! Thank you to Ella Probert and Jamie Gregory for the cover reveal graphics, illustrations and the most stunning cover so far – isn't it gorgeous? And thank you to Julia Bickham for bringing the school to life with her floorplan artwork. Finally, a huge thanks to everyone behind the scenes at Scholastic, from the Rights Team, who have been working their socks off on my behalf, to the people who have been making sure stock of WLKD gets into bookshops around the country. You're all wonderful.

A huge thanks this time must go to each and every school, LEA, bookshop and Council that has invited me to speak at visits and events over the last year. Meeting and talking to readers has been my favourite thing EVER, and I'm always so excited to answer questions and just talk books. Particular thanks to the school staff and students involved in the awards for Last One to Die (the Redhill Trust Book Award 2021/22, The Wirral Book Award 2021/22, The North East Teen Book Award 2021/22, Lancashire Book of the Year 2022 and the RED Book Award 2022) and the YALC team for the best panel ever.

I really hope to see you all again in the future!

Booksellers – you are amazing. Massive thanks to Michelle at Bear Hunt Books for supplying books for my first school visits and giving me coffee and cake. Waterstones, particularly Horsham (Rosie, you're a star), Coventry, Brent Cross and Westfield, you have been magnificent. Thank you for championing Win Lose Kill Die!

Speaking of WLKD, it would be remiss of me not to mention Madison Brooke Williams, who made a little video on TikTok that has had almost two million views. Your love of my book has translated into some of my dreams coming true – thank you for loving it as much as I do!

To the readers. I never thought I'd be signing books, replying to messages or looking at fan art of my characters, but you guys have given me all of that and more. Thank you for your support and I hope you enjoyed my latest sacrifice … er, I mean offering…

To the OG Scribblers – I'm so proud of all of your successes. 2023 is going to be a great year! To Lisa Bradley for helping rewrite the news reports. Apparently, mine had to be rewritten due to "various media law, ethical and regulation reasons". Oops. To Stuart White for double-checking the parts with Ellie's diabetes and giving me first-person insight into the condition. Any mistakes are certainly mine!

To my writing coven (and head witch Georgia). There are too many fabulous women here to name, but you know who you are. Thank you for talking books/writing/drinking wine with me and being wonderful cheerleaders. I'm so pleased to know you all, and the fact that we've been able to meet in real life this year has been such a highlight. Bring on the retreats/down with the patriarchy etc.

To my gorgeous friends and family, especially the ones who buy multiple copies of my books :) Thanks for letting me be an out-and-out weirdo and – even better – being proud of me for it.

To my fab in-laws, it has been a joy spending time together again, from garden parties to dinners at the pub. Alice, you have been so strong and amazing this year and we are all so proud of you. Here's to the future.

My beloved family. Donna – the dedication says it all. Love you. I can't wait to see Danny walk you down that aisle. Kyla and Grayson, you make me such a proud auntie every day. Keep chasing your dreams and being wonderful humans. Mum and Dad, thank you for buying and bragging about my books – your friends must be fed up of you. Keep it up! We will have that retreat by the beach one day. I love you.

Last but never least, Loli and Luke. My little family. I love you so much and I'm excited for everything that comes to us over the next year – it's going to be a good one. Let's go!

MORE CHILLING BOOKS BY CYNTHIA MURPHY: